高职高专创新大学英语系列教材

Creative College English Series

重庆大学出版社

高职高专创新大学英语系列教材 编委会
Creative College English Series

总主审 石 坚 邓 海

总主编 敖 凡 柳吉良 高 红

编写单位（按笔划排序）

乐山职业技术学院	四川大学
四川工商职业技术学院	四川工程职业技术学院
四川天一学院	四川司警职院
四川电力职业技术学院	四川建筑职业技术学院
四川信息职业技术学院	四川省干部函授学院
四川航天职业技术学院	四川烹饪高等专科学校
四川职业技术学院	四川警安职业学院
成都大学	成都艺术职业学院
成都市纺织高等专科学校	成都电子机械高等专科学校
成都农业科技职业学院	成都航空职业技术学院
西华大学	泸州职业技术学院
绵阳职业技术学院	

Creative College
English Series

创新 大学英语 1
STUDENT BOOK

主 编　高　红　　常淑丽　　王朝晖

编 者　高　红　　常淑丽　　王朝晖

　　　　向群英　　曾　剑　　李桂林

　　　　陈宏霞　　赵甜雯

内容提要

《创新大学英语1》是《高职高专创新大学英语系列教材》主教材的第一册。本册含8个单元,每个单元有2篇简短生动的阅读课文,选文涉及校园、社会、文化娱乐等多种题材,时代感强。

每个单元内的练习板块按照 Reading, Speaking, Listening 和 Writing 的顺序安排,既体现了对同一交际主题的反复强化,又可达到学生自然语言输出的目的。每个单元分别覆盖不同的交际主题,强化不同的语法知识,培养不同文体的应用文写作能力。多条线索之间既相互平行,又通过共同训练的高频词汇、共同强调的实际能力以及交际内容与交际形式的有机联系而充分融合在一起,共同服务于提高学生实用交际能力的目标。同时本书还配有多媒体学习光盘,可供学生自学或复习时使用。

图书在版编目(CIP)数据

创新大学英语1/高红等主编. 一重庆:重庆大学出版社,
2008.7
(高职高专创新大学英语系列教材)
ISBN 978-7-5624-4524-1

Ⅰ. 创…　Ⅱ. 高…　Ⅲ. S68　Ⅳ. S68

中国版本图书馆 CIP 数据核字(2008)第 079356 号

创新大学英语1

主编　高　红　常淑丽　王朝晖
责任编辑:向　璐　韩　鹏　版式设计:牟　妮
责任校对:贾　梅　　　　　责任印制:赵　晟

*

重庆大学出版社出版发行
出版人:张鸽盛
社址:重庆市沙坪坝正街 174 号重庆大学(A 区)内
邮编:400030
电话:(023) 65102378　65105781
传真:(023) 65103686　65105565
网址:http://www.cqup.com.cn
邮箱:fxk@ cqup.com.cn(市场营销部)
全国新华书店经销
自贡新华印刷厂印刷

*

开本:787×1092　1/16　印张:9.75　字数:225 千
2008 年 7 月第 1 版　　2008 年 7 月第 1 次印刷
印数:1—8 000
ISBN 978-7-5624-4524-1　定价:24.00 元(含学习光盘)

总 序

目前,国内高职高专院校的大学英语教学改革不断走向深入,"以应用为目的,实用为主,够用为度"的指导原则已经深入人心。在这一背景下,出现了不少各具特色的大学英语教材,它们都不同程度地、从不同的角度反映了新形势下高职院校大学英语教学改革的新思路和课程教学新模式的需要。由于创新型国家的建设与和谐社会的构建不断对高职高专实用创新型人才的培养提出了更高的要求,由于高职高专院校大学英语教学改革不断走向新阶段,开拓出新的层面,也由于高职高专生源的地域差异和学生毕业后所就业的行业差异较大,更好地反映和引导改革中种种新的尝试和新探索的新教材的开发仍然十分必要。

基于这一考虑,重庆大学出版社组织四川省相关领域的专家和 20 多所院校的一线教师,在广泛调研的基础上,编写了这套《高职高专创新大学英语系列教材》。参与教材编写的既有教育部在该地区重点高校的骨干教师,也有长期在高职高专教学一线的骨干教师。

本教材以教育部《高职高专教育英语课程教学基本要求》为依据,以四川省和其他西部省市的高职高专教育以及大学英语教育的实际为出发点,以"打好基础,注重培养实际使用语言的技能,特别是使用英语处理日常和涉外业务活动的能力"为原则,以"实用为主,够用为度"为编写指导思想,使本套教材具有以下特点:

(1)着眼于培养技术、生产、管理和服务等领域的高等应用性专门人才的实际需求,强调学生的基础知识的扎实掌握和基本能力的充分训练,注重培养学生的语言应用能力,特别是实用口语和实用写作等方面的交际能力。

(2)将学生的应用性交际能力的培养融汇在基本技能的雕琢中,充分体现"双基"教学的需要;让学生充分扎实地掌握大纲所规定的知识和能力,强调学以致用和学用结合。

（3）以高频词汇贯穿听说读写译的基本技能训练之中，不一味追求教材梯度，强调通过高频词汇的反复综合训练，提升学生的语感，培养其实际语言交际能力。

（4）学习材料短小精炼，练习形式丰富多样，着眼于对词汇的积极运用能力的培养，通过对传统练习模式的突破来带动教学理念的改变。

（5）在体例编排上充分考虑学生的自主学习能力的提高，促进学生的自我发展。

（6）在练习设计和教材体系上注重课内外学习的有机结合，充分利用学生课外的时间，既方便教师对学生的课外学习进行有效的管理和监控，又服务于丰富第二课堂和提高学生文化素质的需要。

（7）有完善的立体开发体系，这种立体开发既体现于载体形式的丰富性，也体现在不同载体形式在内容上的互补性，而不是相同内容的简单重复，从而使教材的立体开发和课内外学习的配合相得益彰。

《高职高专创新大学英语系列教材》由主教材《创新大学英语》、《创新大学英语教师用书》和《创新大学英语综合训练》各4册组成，并配有相应的多媒体学习课件和电子教案。

《创新大学英语》每册含8个单元，每个单元有2篇简短生动的阅读课文，在每个单元内，为了实现 input 对于 output 的引导，练习板块按照"Reading"，"Speaking"，"Listening"和"Writing"的顺序安排，既体现了对同一交际主题的反复强化又使得学生的语言输出"水到渠成"，"顺理成章"。在单元之间的关系上，每个单元分别覆盖不同的交际主题，强化不同的语法知识，培养不同文体的应用文写作能力。多条线索之间既相互平行，又通过共同训练的高频词汇、共同强调的实际能力以及交际内容与交际形式的有机联系而充分融合在一起，共同服务于提高学生实用交际能力这一目标。同时本书还配有多媒体学习光盘，可供学生自学或复习时使用。

《创新大学英语综合训练》中每一单元由 Micro-skills Practice 和 Comprehensive Skills and Practice 两部分组成，前者包括 Vocabulary 和 Sentence Pattern 两个板块，后者包括 Listening, Speaking, Reading for Skill, Translation 和 Writing 等板块。《综合训练》在练习的词汇、强化的语法点与训练的交际形式上与学生用书保持一致，但在训练的量、练习的形式以及阅读技巧的培养上又有所拓展，教师可根据需要灵活选择布置给学生练习，这既体现了课内学习和课外学习的有机结合,又扩大了本系列教材的适用面。

《创新大学英语教师用书》除了提供基本的练习答案和课文翻译以外,既有课文的相关背景知识介绍、长难句分析、词汇和语法点讲解,又有语法和构词法方面的专题知识、阅读技巧分析、写作词汇拓展和实用文写作常识简介,内容极为丰富,教师可以根据学生的实际需要对症下药,灵活选取讲解内容。同时《教师用书》还配有教学课件光盘,方便老师备课和组织课堂教学活动。

由于本系列教材有上述种种新颖之处,因此在推出之后将为四川省和西部其他省区公共英语教学改革做出独特的贡献,在提高学生实用英语交际能力的同时也为高职高专大学教材的编写和大学英语的教学开展了一定的创新尝试。

因为本系列教材在许多方面都进行了新的尝试,在实际编写过程中可能会出现一些疏漏和不当之处,请各位老师、专家和读者批评指正并将相关意见和建议及时反馈给我们,以促进本教材的进一步完善。

总主编
2008 年 5 月

编写说明

　　本教材为《高职高专创新大学英语》系列教材的学生用书第 1 册,从板块的设计到内容的选择都力求体现该系列教材"以应用为目的,实用为主,够用为度"的指导原则。

　　全书共含 8 个单元,每个单元由 7 个板块构成。各板块的侧重点互不相同,但在内容上相互关联,在知识上和语言上相互支撑,形成一个整体,以达到学以致用、讲练结合的目的。此外,本书特别加入了有关文化背景知识的介绍,以帮助学生在实际运用英语进行交际中能更得体地使用语言,从而实现《高职高专教育英语课程教学基本要求》所要求的"强调打好语言基础和培养语言应用能力并重;语言基本技能的训练和培养实际从事涉外交际活动的语言应用能力并重"的目标。

　　本书的第一个板块为阅读。该板块围绕一篇既贴近学生生活,又富有文化内涵的短文展开,并配以阅读理解练习、词汇学习、句型转换和英汉翻译练习。目的是使学生通过阅读和相关练习,逐步培养综合归纳的能力、理解和运用英语词汇的能力及熟悉和灵活运用英语的表达方式和句型的能力,并掌握基本的汉译英、英译汉的技巧,使翻译更准确、更符合中英文的习惯。

　　第二板块为会话。该板块包括 4 个部分:注意事项、常用句型,对话范文及情景对话练习。目的是在增加交际中语言多样性的同时,唤起学生对跨文化交际中的语言和文化差异的关注,提高交际的得体性。

　　第三个板块为听力。听力是外语学习的必备能力之一,也是难点之一。鉴于在造成听力困难的诸多原因中,语言的生疏和文化背景的不足扮演着重要的角色,本教材特意将听力板块置于会话之后,听力的内容与会话相关。其目的一方面是为了降低听力的难度,缓解学生听力中的焦虑感,使听力训练变得更轻松、更具有成效;同时听力训练又为会话提供了更多的范文,使二者相互支撑,互为补充。

第四个板块为发音练习及拼写规则。目的是帮助学生巩固和进一步学习英语单音及其在连续话语中的发音,并进一步熟悉发音与拼写的关系,以帮助学生摆脱记单词难的问题。该部分还特意选择了谚语、小诗、笑话、谜语作例句以增加知识性和趣味性。

第五个板块为语法练习。本书从第一册起,每个单元对大纲所要求的主要语法现象逐一进行专项练习。练习以各语法现象的重难点为主,以帮助学生发现问题,巩固已有的语法知识。

第六个板块为写作。本册写作练习以信息(描写)功能为主,每个单元都包括一个日常短文写作。该部分的写作题目与该单元前几个板块的内容密切相关,目的是要求学生将课文中所学单词、句型用于写作中,写出连贯、正确的句子,并掌握英语段落写作的一些基本特点。此外,在每个奇数单元中,还包含有一个应用文写作练习。本册书所要求的应用文写作练习包括:问候卡、明信片、书信,短信等,目的是使学生掌握一些基本的交际技能。

本书的最后一个板块为一篇短文阅读。其目的是使学习者通过阅读增加词汇量,扩大视野,并掌握基本的阅读技巧。

《高职高专创新大学英语》系列教材学生用书第一册总主编为敖凡、柳吉良和高红。第一册主编为高红、常淑丽和王朝晖。参加编写的人员有高红,常淑丽、王朝晖、向群英、曾剑、李桂林、陈宏霞、赵甜雯,分别负责第一至第八单元的编写。石坚、邓海审定,在此一并表示感谢。

编者

2008 年 7 月

Contents

Unit I. Learning English

TEXT A　　American Small Talk

When Americans meet one another for the first time, they begin their conversation with "small talk". The **topics** of these conversations are very **general** and often **situational**—people **start** talking about anything in their **common physical environment**, such as the **weather**, the room in which they are **standing**, the food that they are eating, etc. Small talk is important because Americans are not very **comfortable** with **silence**. It is important, however, to know which topics are **acceptable** and which are **unacceptable** in American **culture**.

Situational topics like the weather are acceptable in many cultures, but they **obviously** cannot be discussed for a long **period** of time. Asking someone about his/her **occupation** is also very common, **especially** for Americans, who place a high **value** on working. Questions of **taste** could also be asked. **Compliments** are common conversation **starters**. Last, in a country like **the United States** where people **move** so often, places of **origin** are often discussed as well.

There are many topics, however, that are **inappropriate** to use in starting a conversation. For example, **religion** is **considered** a very **personal** matter. **Politics** is usually another unacceptable topic. Two other **subjects** will **immediately** make Americans **uncomfortable**: age and money. Americans value **youth**, so many Americans would want to **keep** their age a **secret**. **Regarding financial** matters, **income** and the price of **possessions** are also personal matters and should not be used to start a conversation with an American.

Being aware of these acceptable and unacceptable topics may help people from other cultures feel more comfortable around Americans they are meeting for the first time. Listening to American small talk has often led non-natives to make wrong judgments about an American's ability to carry on a conversation. Culture, however, influences the way that people communicate with one another. Learning about this feature of conversation will help you understand Americans better.

(307 words)

New Words

American	/əˈmerɪkən/	a.	美国的;美洲的
		n.	美国人;美洲人
★topic	/ˈtɒpɪk/	n.	话题,题目;主题
general	/ˈdʒenrəl/	a.	一般的;普遍的
situational	/ˌsɪtʃuˈeɪʃnəl/	a.	情景的,环境的
start	/ˈstɑːt/	v.	开始
common	/ˈkɒmən/	a.	常见的;共同的
physical	/ˈfɪzɪkl/	a.	客观存在的,现实的
environment	/ɪnˈvaɪrənmənt/	n.	环境,自然环境
weather	/ˈweðə/	n.	天气
stand	/stænd/	v.	站立
comfortable	/ˈkʌmftəbl/	a.	舒服的
silence	/ˈsaɪləns/	n.	沉默;寂静
acceptable	/əkˈseptəbl/	a.	可接受的;认同的,认可的
unacceptable	/ˌʌnəkˈseptəbl/	a.	不能接受的
culture	/ˈkʌltʃə/	n.	文化
obviously	/ˈɒbviəsli/	ad.	显然,明显地
period	/ˈpɪəriəd/	n.	一段时间
occupation	/ˌɒkjuˈpeɪʃn/	n.	职业,工作
especially	/ɪˈspeʃəli/	ad.	尤其,特别
★value	/ˈvæljuː/	n.	重要性,价值　v. 重视
★taste	/teɪst/	n.	爱好,喜好;味道
▲compliment	/ˈkɒmplɪmənt/	n.	问候;称赞
starter	/ˈstɑːtə/	n.	开端,由头
▲move	/muːv/	v.	搬迁;移动

origin	/ˈɒrɪdʒɪn/	*n.*	出身;起源
★inappropriate	/ˌɪnəˈprəupriət/	*a.*	不合适的,不恰当的
religion	/rɪˈlɪdʒən/	*n.*	宗教;宗教信仰
consider	/kənˈsɪdə/	*v.*	认为,觉得
personal	/ˈpɜːsənl/	*a.*	个人的,私人的
politics	/ˈpɒlətɪks/	*n.*	政治,政治事务
subject	/ˈsʌbdʒɪkt/	*n.*	话题,主题;学科,科目
immediately	/ɪˈmiːdiətli/	*ad.*	立刻,立即
uncomfortable	/ʌnˈkʌmftəbl/	*a.*	使人不舒服的
youth	/juːθ/	*n.*	年轻,青春;青年时期;男青年
keep	/kiːp/	*v.*	保留,保存;使保持,使继续
secret	/ˈsiːkrət/	*n.*	秘密
regarding	/rɪˈgɑːdɪŋ/	*prep.*	关于,至于
★financial	/faɪˈnænʃl/	*a.*	财政的,金融的
income	/ˈɪnkʌm/	*n.*	收入
possession	/pəˈzeʃn/	*n.* [*usu. pl.*]	个人财产,私有物品;拥有

Phrases and Expressions

one another	相互
to begin with	从…开始,以…为起点
talk about	谈论,谈话
such as	例如,诸如
be comfortable with	与…相处感觉自在;在…方面自信而无忧虑
place a high value on	对…极为重视
as well	也,同样
for example	例如
be aware of	觉察到,知道
lead somebody to do something	导致…做…
carry on	继续做,坚持干

Proper Names

the United States	美国

课文词数	生词总量	生词比率	二级词汇	三级词汇	超纲词汇
307	41	13.4%	34	5	2

GETTING THE MESSAGE

I. Recite the first two paragraphs of the text.

II. Decide which of the following best states the main idea of the passage.

A. Small talk differs from one situation to another.

B. There are acceptable and unacceptable topics for American small talk.

C. The topics of small talk are very general.

D. Small talk is important in communication.

III. Answer the following questions.

1. What is American small talk? Why is it so important in American culture?

2. What are the topics common in American small talk?

3. What are the topics unacceptable in American small talk?

4. As far as you know, what is the common way for Chinese people to greet each other now?

VOCABULARY AND STRUCTURE

I. Match words or phrases in Column A with their explanations in Column B.

A	B
1. be aware of	a. a complete lack of noise or sound
2. immediately	b. the condition of temperature, wind, rain, sunshine, etc. at a certain time
3. consider	c. a subject for conversation, talk, writing, etc.
4. silence	d. the period of being young
5. occupation	e. anxious, embarrassed or afraid and unable to relax
6. weather	f. to change the place where you live, have your work, etc.
7. uncomfortable	g. to think about sth. carefully in order to make a decision
8. topic	h. at once
9. move	i. a job
10. youth	j. to know or realize sth.

II. Fill in the blank in each sentence with a word or phrase taken from the box below. Change the word form if necessary.

such as	like	and	be comfortable with
for example	but	special	however

1. This pair of shoes is made _____ for you.
2. She _____ more _____ computer than with people.
3. I'm sorry, _____ I won't be able to come tonight.
4. What's your new job _____?
5. Noise, _____, is a kind of pollution as well.
6. I have been to many places, _____ Beijing, Shanghai, Guangdong, etc.

III. Rewrite the following sentences after the model.

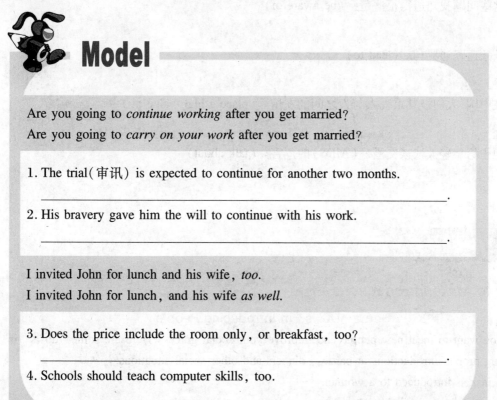

Model

Are you going to *continue working* after you get married?
Are you going to *carry on your work* after you get married?

1. The trial(审讯) is expected to continue for another two months.
   _____.

2. His bravery gave him the will to continue with his work.
   _____.

I invited John for lunch and his wife, *too.*
I invited John for lunch, and his wife *as well.*

3. Does the price include the room only, or breakfast, too?
   _____.

4. Schools should teach computer skills, too.
   _____.

IV. Translate the following sentences into Chinese.

1. The topics of these conversations are very general and often situational—people start talking about anything in their common physical environment, such as the weather, the room in which they are standing, the food that they are eating, etc.

2. Asking someone about his/her occupation is also very common, especially for Americans, who place a high value on working.

3. Being aware of these acceptable and unacceptable topics may help people from other cultures feel more comfortable around Americans they are meeting for the first time.

V. Translate the following sentences with words or phrases learnt in Text A.

1. 人们第一次相遇时通常要相互打招呼。(for the first time)

2. 这些问题我知道得很清楚。(be aware of)

3. 条条道路通罗马。(lead to)

4. 在中国,人们极其重视人与人之间的友谊。(place a high value on)

5. 他想给年轻人谈谈艾滋病(AIDS)的危害。(talk about)

Speaking

I. How to Make Introductions

Some "DO's" in Introducing People

Do you want to meet new people and improve your social graces? Here are some "do's" in making proper introductions at parties, dinners and other social situations.

☺ A man is introduced to a woman.

☺ A younger person is introduced to an older one.

☺ An unmarried woman is introduced to a married woman.

☺ A person in a lower social position is introduced to one in a higher position.

☺ An individual is introduced to the group first, then the group to the individual. But if an

introduction is made in the house, the family member is introduced to the guest first.

☺ Do comment briefly on the backgrounds, when introducing two people. Comment on some hobby or interest common to both.

☺ If your host neglects to introduce you to other guests, feel free to introduce yourself, but make your relationship to the host clear in your introduction.

Useful Sentences	
Hi, I'm Mary. Mary, this is Jane.	Nice/Good/Glad/Pleased to meet you.
I don't believe we've met before. I'm...	Hi. I'm...
I'd like you to meet Mr... I'd like to introduce you to Mr... Allow me to introduce Mr... May I introduce you to Mr...	It's a pleasure to meet you. Very glad to meet you. How do you do?

Model

Huang Min: A nice party, isn't it?

Silver: Yes. I'm enjoying it very much.

Huang Min: By the way, I'm Huang Min, a freshman majoring in computer science.

Silver: Glad to meet you.

Huang Min: So am I. May I have your name?

Silver: Elizabeth Silver. But please call me Elizabeth.

Huang Min: Sorry, what's your last name again? Sliver?

Silver: Actually, it's Silver.

Huang Min: How do you spell that?

Silver: S-I-L-V-E-R.

II. How to Greet People

Useful Sentence Patterns		
Good Morning. Good afternoon. Good evening. Hi! Hello!		Good Morning. Good afternoon. Good evening. Hi! Hello!
Good Morning. Good afternoon. Good evening.	How are you?	Very well, thank you. How are you? Fine, thank you. And you?
Hi! Hello!	How are things going? How's it going? How're you doing? How are you getting along?	Fine, thanks. And you? Great! What about you? Pretty good, thank you. Fine! How are things with you?

Model

Huang Min: Hey, Elizabeth. How's it going?

Silver:　　Fine, thanks. What about you?

Huang Min: Pretty good. So, are your classes interesting this term?

Silver:　　Yes, very interesting. I really like computer programming.

Huang Min: Computer programming? But I think it's a bit difficult for me. Listen, I'm on my way to the library. Are you on your way to the class?

Silver:　　No, my class today is in the afternoon. I'm going to the library, too.

Huang Min: Oh, really? Let's go.

III. Practice

1. Complete the following conversations and then act them out in pairs.

1) Liu Qian met an old schoolmate of hers on campus.

Liu Qian: _____, Wang Mei. I haven't seen you for a long time. _____?

Wang Mei: Pretty good, thank you. _____?

Liu Qian: Just OK. Only we have too much spare time here. What do you like to do in your spare time?

Wang Mei: Sometimes, I _____ the library. _____, I just _____ to music or do some sports.

Liu Qian: That's interesting. _____?

Wang Mei: I'm heading for the bookshop.

Liu Qian: Oh, really? I'm going to the post office, the same direction. Let's go together.

Wang Mei: _____.

2) At a welcome party, Zhou Yong met lots of new faces. She went up and tried to talk with them.

Zhou Yong: Hello, _____ Zhou Yong, a freshman from Class 2.

Li Jiao: I'm Li Jiao, a sophomore from Class 1. _____.

Zhou Yong: Nice to meet you, too. So _____?

Li Jiao: I'm from Chongqing. _____?

Zhou Yong: I'm from Yunnan. _____?

Li Jiao: Yes, I've been to Lijiang, with my family. Lijiang is really a very wonderful place. Actually, it's one of the most beautiful places I've ever been to.

Zhou Yong: I can't agree with you more.

2. Work in Pairs. Practise greeting with your partner according to the situations below. Then switch roles.

1) Mr. Li, a freshman, meets Mr. Wang, who comes from the same native town. They greet each other and talk about their university life and studies.

2) At a dancing party, you run into many people you don't know. Try to start a conversation with someone you don't know and talk about something both of you are interested in.

B Listening

Listen to the four conversations and choose the best answer to each question you hear.

1. A. A friend of Alex Lam. B. Alex's sister. C. Mary's sister.
2. A. Mary Nielson.   B. Mary Nelson. C. Mary Neilson.
3. A. It's awful.   B. Not too bad.   C. Very pleasant.
4. A. Africa.   B. Ankara.   C. America.
5. A. Bob's friend.   B. John's friend. C. John's girl friend.
6. A. Bob.   B. John.   C. Barbara.
7. A. Linda is Susan's niece, and Mr. Peterson's friend.
 B. Susan is Linda's niece, and Mr. Peterson's friend.
 C. Susan is Linda's aunt, and Mr. Peterson's friend.
8. A. Yes, but only a little.
 B. Yes, she has heard a lot about him.
 C. No, she has never heard about him before.

C Sounds and Spellings

I. Listen and practise. Pay special attention to the pronunciation of the italicized letters.

1. /p/	slee*p*
2. /b/	*b*e
3. /t/	*t*ime, le*tt*er, work*ed*
4. /d/	*d*o, stay*ed*, mi*dd*le
5. /k/	boo*k*, bla*ck*, *c*ook, ac*c*use, *ch*aracter
6. /g/	*g*o, *gu*ard

II. Listen and practise. Pay special attention to the pronunciation of the plosives in continuous speech.

1. A word spoken is an arrow let fly.　一言既出,驷马难追。
2. Pain is gain.　痛苦即是收获。
3. Dogs do not eat dogs.　同行不该是冤家。
4. Better be poor than wicked.　宁可一贫如洗,决不为非作歹。
5. Speech is silver, silence is gold.　雄辩是银,缄默是金。

III. Read and enjoy.

A：What word is always spelled incorrectly? B：Incorrectly.　　　　　　　　　　☺☺☺☺☺

D Grammar

I. Fill in the blanks with the words given and change the form of them when necessary.

1. I saw two _____ and two _____ talking excitedly in front of the canteen. (Chinese, America)

2. There are a lot of _____ down there but hardly any _____. (sheep, people)

3. Pass me two _____ of _____, please. (piece, paper)

4. These _____ books sell well in the bookstore. (child + story)

5. Mon bought a lot of _____ yesterday. (potato)

6. This pair of _____ is nice. (shoe)

7. _____ turn yellow in autumn. (leaf)

8. Here are some _____ of my family. (photo)

9. These _____ are heavy. (box)

10. We like _____ very much, so we grow some in our _____ garden every year. (vegetable, vegetable)

II. *Choose the one that best completes the sentence among the four choices marked A , B , C and D below each sentence.*

1. All the _____ in the hospital got a rise yesterday.

   A. women doctors   B. woman doctors

   C. women doctor   D. woman doctor

2. After ten years, all those youngsters became _____.

   A. growns-ups   B. growns-up

   C. grown-up   D. grown-ups

3. _____ grazing on the meadow.

   A. The cattle was   B. The cattles were

   C. The cattle were   D. A cattle was

4. The young couple bought _____ for their new house.

   A. a lot of new furniture   B. some new furnitures

   C. many new furniture   D. many new furnitures

5. He arrived at the hotel, but his baggage _____ still on the way.

   A. was   B. were

   C. get   D. had been

6. Could you show me the way to the _____ shop?

   A. shoes'   B. shoes

   C. shoe's   D. shoe

7. His article is better than _____ in his class.

   A. anyone's else   B. anyone else

   C. anyone's else's   D. anyone else's

8. The pretty girl in pink over there is _____.

   A. a friend of my   B. a friend of mine

   C. a friend of I   D. mine friend

9. _____ are going to Singapore for a holiday.

   A. The Wangs   B. The Wang

   C. Wang's   D. The Wang's

10. The woman over there is _____.

    A. Jenny and Linda mother   B. Jenny and Linda's mother

    C. Jenny's and Linda's mother   D. Jenny and Lindas' mother

Writing

I. General Writing

Read the following passage and then write a brief introduction to one of your classmates without mentioning his/her name. You are required to read it aloud in class next time and see if your classmates can guess who he/she is.

My best friend comes from Chongqing. She is a pretty girl with a round face and two big dark eyes. She is about 1.60 meters tall and always has a smile on her face. She has many hobbies, such as dancing, listening to pop music, and playing computer games, but her favourite hobby is drawing, because she likes all the different colours.

Now can you guess who she is?

II. Writing for Specific Purposes

Read the following sample and then write a greeting card to one of your friends. It can be a card for a holiday, birthday, anniversary or any other occasions, using expressions such as:

Congratulations (on...)!

Happy birthday/anniversary (to)...!

Best wishes (for/on...)!

Tips for Writing

Greeting Cards

Most of us enjoy getting greeting cards from time to time. Birthdays, anniversaries, holidays, the birth of a baby, and other occasions mean even more to us when we are remembered by friends, relatives and colleagues. A greeting card usually includes:

- Name of the recipient
- The message
- Name of the sender

Be sure that the "To" before the name of the recipient should be capitalized while the "from" before the name of the sender is in lower case.

Sample

TO Mr. and Mrs. Peterson,

Merry Christmas!

May your home be filled with happiness…
your hearts with love…
your days with joy…

from Li Yong & Zhang Qian

TEXT B — Successful English Learning

Research in the field of language **indicates** that there are many things you can do to become a successful language learner. **Curiosity** about language and culture, daily study, and the **commitment** to use English in every possible situation while in an English-speaking environment, are very important **conditions** for **success**.

Be clear and realistic about your goals.

Know what your goals are. Do you need English for **occasional** speaking situations? Do you want to **improve comprehension** in both written and spoken English? Do you need to write English for **professional purposes**? There are many reasons to learn English, and your reasons are your own goals.

Be realistic about the length of time it takes to learn a language.

Programs which **promise overnight** success are **simply** not being honest. Language learning is a **cumulative** progress. You will notice **improvement** at different **speeds** in each **skill** area. Many students progress more quickly in **passive** skill areas (reading and grammar **analysis**) than in **active** and **complex** skill areas (speaking, note-taking **during** a lecture).

Learn something about "language learning".

Remember that language is a complex **system** of **meaningful** sounds **organized** with a **series** of rules（grammar）. Every student has to study enough **pronunciation**, grammar and sentence structure to understand this！It is also true that language is a form of **behaviour involving** the human need to **communicate** and to be understood. Language learning involves **motivation**, **emotion**, a **sense** of self and a set of **cultural beliefs**. Language is much more than sound and words and grammar. Language learning **requires** that you make **mistakes**. Do not be afraid of a language or afraid of making **errors**. **Develop** an ability to **relax**；"playing" with a new language is an important part of learning.

（292 words）

New Words

successful	/sək'sesfl/	*a.*	达到目的的，获得成功的
research	/rɪ'sɜːtʃ/	*n.*	研究，调查
indicate	/'ɪndɪkeɪt/	*v.*	表明，显示
curiosity	/ˌkjuəri'ɔsəti/	*n.*	好奇心，求知欲
★commitment	/kə'mɪtmənt/	*n.*	承诺，许诺
condition	/kən'dɪʃn/	*n.*	环境，状态，条件；［*pl.*］状态，状况
success	/sək'ses/	*n.*	成功
realistic	/riːə'lɪstɪk/	*a.*	现实的，实际的，实事求是的
★occasional	/ə'keɪʒənl/	*a.*	偶尔的，临时的
improve	/ɪm'pruːv/	*v.*	改进，改善
comprehension	/ˌkɒmprɪ'henʃn/	*n.*	理解力，领悟能力
★professional	/prə'feʃənl/	*a.*	职业的，专业的
purpose	/'pɜːpəs/	*n.*	目的，用途
take	/teɪk/	*v.*	需要（一段时间），（费时）；携带，拿走
program	/'prəugræm/	*n.*	计划，方案，大纲
promise	/'prɒmɪs/	*v.*	许诺，承诺
▲overnight	/ˌəuvə'naɪt/	*ad.*	突然，一夜之间
simply	/'sɪmpli/	*ad.*	（强调某说法）确实，简直；（强调简单）仅仅，只
▲cumulative	/'kjuːmjulətɪv/	*a.*	累积的，累计的
improvement	/ɪm'pruːvmənt/	*n.*	改善，改进

speed	/spiːd/	n.	速度
skill	/skɪl/	n.	技能;技艺
passive	/ˈpæsɪv/	a.	被动的;消极的
analysis	/əˈnæləsɪs/	n.	分析;分析结果
active	/ˈæktɪv/	a.	积极的,活跃的
★complex	/ˈkɒmpleks/	a.	复杂的,难懂的
during	/ˈdjuərɪŋ/	prep.	在…期间
remember	/rɪˈmembə/	v.	记住;记得
system	/ˈsɪstəm/	n.	体系;系统
meaningful	/ˈmiːnɪŋfl/	a.	具有重要意义的
organize	/ˈɔːgənaɪz/	v.	组织
series	/ˈsɪəriːz/	n.	一系列
pronunciation	/prəˌnʌnsiˈeɪʃn/	n.	发音,读音
behaviour	/bɪˈheɪvjə/	n.	行为,举止
involve	/ɪnˈvɒlv/	v.	牵涉;包含
communicate	/kəˈmjuːnɪkeɪt/	v.	交流;传,传递(想法、感情、思想等)
motivation	/ˌməutɪˈveɪʃn/	n.	动机
emotion	/ɪˈməuʃn/	n.	情感,情绪
sense	/sens/	n.	意识;感官;感觉
cultural	/ˈkʌltʃərəl/	a.	文化的,与文化有关的
belief	/bɪˈliːf/	n.	信念,信仰;相信
require	/rɪˈkwaɪə/	v.	需要,依靠
mistake	/mɪˈsteɪk/	n.	错误,失误
error	/ˈerə/	n.	错误,差错
develop	/dɪˈveləp/	v.	发展,开发
relax	/rɪˈlæks/	v.	放松,休息

课文词数	生词总量	生词比率	二级词汇	三级词汇	超纲词汇
292	46	15.8%	40	4	2

Judge , according to the text , whether the following statements are True or False.

1. _____ Using the skills of language learning will help you succeed.
2. _____ If you want to learn English well, it's not important to know your goals.
3. _____ Your English learning may be an overnight success if you have good methods.
4. _____ Your improvement in reading and speaking will be at the same speed.
5. _____ Language learning doesn't only involve vocabulary, grammar and sentence structure.

Unit 2 Higher Education

Some of my best and **favorite memories** come from college. **Growing** up in a small town, I sometimes felt **stuck**. I **ended** up going to college in a small town, too, though. It didn't matter. I made **wonderful** friends there, but most **importantly**, I learned a lot about myself.

College **really provides** you with a time to **figure** out what your **interests** are. Even if you're already **aware** of your interests, it **lets** you **continue** to **narrow** them down **until** you can start to **shape** them into a **career**. You can **choose** your classes and, for the most part, can **avoid** subject matter that isn't **appealing** to you. Because I had chosen a small **liberal arts** school, I got to know my **professors** really well. Even now, two years after I've **graduated**, they still remember me with great **detail** and ask how teaching is going, even though I never told them I was teaching. They just knew that's what I was planning on doing. It's a good feeling.

Because you spend so much time around others in college, you make really strong and **lasting** friendships because, **essentially**, you're living together and you're part of the same **community**. It's really nice to have that kind of **support** system, especially as you're getting used to being away from home and away from your family.

The best thing that college does is to **prepare** you for the real world. Each year of college is another year of **independence gained**. Each year you learn a little more about yourself and what you're **capable** of. When you come in, you're really just a big high **schooler**. When you go out, you're an **adult** with goals and a career and you're ready to **actually** make it in the world.

Many high schoolers say that they have no interest in going to college because their idea of schooling is based on the **prison** that is the **secondary education** system. They need to know that college is so, so much more than that and that it is **definitely** a **worthwhile experience**, **educationally, socially, and personally.**

(352 words)

New Words

favorite	/ˈfeɪvərɪt/	a.	特别受喜爱的
memory	/ˈmeməri/	n.	回忆;记忆力
grow	/grəʊ/	v.	成长;扩大
stuck	/stʌk/	a.	困窘的,迷惑的;卡住的,困住的
end	/end/	v.	结束;断绝
wonderful	/ˈwʌndəfl/	a.	很好的;精彩的
importantly	/ɪmˈpɔːtntli/	ad.	重要地
really	/ˈriːəli/	ad.	确实;真正地
provide	/prəˈvaɪd/	v.	提供;给予
figure	/ˈfɪgə/	v.	明白,理解;估计,判断
interest	/ˈɪntrəst/	n.	兴趣;利益
aware	/əˈweə/	a.	知道的,意识到的
let	/let/	v.	让;允许
continue	/kənˈtɪnjuː/	v.	继续做;持续
narrow	/ˈnærəʊ/	v.	缩小;使局限于
until	/ənˈtɪl/	conj.	直到…为止;到…时
shape	/ʃeɪp/	v.	塑造;使成为…形状(样子)
★career	/kəˈrɪə/	n.	职业;事业
choose	/tʃuːz/	v.	选择,挑选
avoid	/əˈvɔɪd/	v.	避免,避开
★appealing	/əˈpiːlɪŋ/	a.	吸引人的

▲liberal arts			文科
professor	/prəˈfesə/	n.	教授
graduate	/ˈɡrædʒuət/	v.	大学毕业;毕业
		n.	(大学)毕业生;研究生
detail	/ˈdiːteɪl/	n.	细节;细微之处
lasting	/ˈlɑːstɪŋ/	a.	持久的;永恒的
★essentially	/ɪˈsenʃəli/	ad.	根本上;本质上
community	/kəˈmjuːnəti/	n.	群体;社区
support	/səˈpɔːt/	n.	帮助;支持 v.支持
prepare	/prɪˈpeə/	v.	准备
independence	/ˌɪndɪˈpendəns/	n.	独立,自立
gain	/ɡeɪn/	v.	获得;增加
capable	/ˈkeɪpəbl/	a.	有能力的;能的
schooler	/skuːlə/	n.	学生
adult	/ˈædʌlt/	n.	成年人
actually	/ˈæktʃuəli/	ad.	确实;实际上
prison	/ˈprɪzn/	n.	监狱
★secondary	/ˈsekəndri/	a.	中级的;中等教育的;次要的
education	/ˌedʒuˈkeɪʃn/	n.	教育
definitely	/ˈdefɪnətli/	ad.	肯定;明确地
★worthwhile	/ˌwɜːθˈwaɪl/	a.	值得努力的,值得(做)的;重要的
experience	/ɪkˈspɪəriəns/	n.	经历;体验
educationally	/ˌedʒuˈkeɪʃənli/	ad.	在教育方面
socially	/ˈsəuʃli/	ad.	在社交方面
personally	/ˈpɜːsənəli/	ad.	就本人而言;亲自

Phrases and Expressions

grow up	长大,成长
end up	最终成为;最后处于
make friends	结交朋友
provide...with	为…提供
figure out	弄明白,想出
even if	即使,虽然
narrow down	缩小,限制

shape...into	将…塑造为,使…形成
for the most part	通常,总的来说
subject matter	主要内容,题材
liberal arts	文科
even though	即使,尽管
get used to	适应于,习惯于
be capable of	有能力;有才能
make it	成功
be based on	以…为基础

课文词数	生词总量	生词比率	二级词汇	三级词汇	超纲词汇
352	46	13.1%	40	5	1

GETTING THE MESSAGE

I. Recite the second paragraph of the text.

II. Decide which of the following best states the main idea of the passage.

A. The author figures out why college life is greatly different from high school life.

B. The best reason to go to college is to learn more about the world you live in.

C. College education is worthwhile because it leads to your personal growth.

D. College years cannot be forgotten easily.

III. Answer the following questions.

1. What do you want to gain from college education?

2. Why can you make wonderful friends in college?

3. What is the best thing that college does?

4. How do you benefit from college education?

VOCABULARY AND STRUCTURE

I. Match words or phrases in Column A with their explanations in Column B.

A	B
1. detail	a. to come finally to a particular place or position
2. worthwhile	b. continuing for a long time
3. support	c. to get a degree from a university or college
4. narrow	d. worth spending time, money or effort on
5. end up	e. a fully grown person
6. lasting	f. to place or establish on a base or basis
7. adult	g. a small individual fact or item
8. capable	h. to reduce the number of possibilities or choices
9. graduate	i. having the ability necessary for doing sth.
10. base on	j. to give or be ready to give help to sb. if they need it

II. Fill in the blank in each sentence with a word or phrase taken from the box below. Change the word form if necessary.

figure out	gain	experience	narrow
essentially	lasting	base on	end up

1. People hope that a _____ peace will be established in this region.
2. The boy has to _____ his hobby to basketball because he should spend more time on study.
3. Work _____ helps you to find out what a career in your chosen field would be like.
4. If you always waste money like that, you'll _____ in debt.
5. A good marriage is _____ trust.
6. He's _____ a very generous man.

III. Rewrite the following sentences after the model.

Model

His friend *provided* him *with* funds to run a store.
His friend *provided* funds *for* him to run a store.

1. The company aims to *provide* the market *with* green energy.

   _____.

2. These websites will *provide* us *with* all the information we need.

   _____.

Growing up in a small town, I sometimes felt stuck.
Because I grew up in a small town, I sometimes felt stuck.

3. *Being excited*, I couldn't go to sleep.

   _____.

4. *Reading so attentively*, he forgot the time for lunch.

   _____.

IV. Translate the following sentences into Chinese.

1. Some of my best and favorite memories come from college.
2. Even if you're already aware of your interests, it lets you continue to narrow them down until you can start to shape them into a career.
3. The best thing that college does is to prepare you for the real world.

V. Translate the following sentences with words or phrases learnt in Text A.

1. 他正在努力想办法解决这个问题。(figure out)

2. 只有人类才是能使用工具的动物吗？(capable of)

3. 他们把结论建立在事实的基础上。(base on)

4. 没有家人的支持,他大学是毕不了业的。(support, graduate)

5. 我不习惯晚上这么迟吃饭。（get used to）

 **Speaking**

I. How to Say Goodbye

Saying goodbye is never easy. There are many different ways to say good-bye to someone, with shortened versions of these as well. However, there are also extra elements that can be added to your good-bye for you to achieve the full effect. Also, almost any emotion can be expressed with your good-bye.

Useful Sentences

1. Excuse me, I'm afraid I have to go now / I won't be able to stay any longer.

> See you later. / See you next time.
>
> Goodbye. / Bye-bye.
>
> So long.
>
> See you around.
>
> Take care.
>
> Until we meet again.
>
> Stay in touch.
>
> All the best.

2. It's a pity for us to see you go / We're sorry you have to leave, and I'll look forward to...

> seeing you soon.
>
> hearing from you soon.
>
> visiting you very soon.

3. Take care of yourself and don't forget to ...

> write to me.
>
> give us a call.
>
> keep in touch.

Model

Zhang Hua:	Jason, I'm calling to say goodbye.
Jason:	How time flies! When are you off?
Zhang Hua:	Tomorrow afternoon.
Jason:	We'll miss you. Hope to see you again soon.
Zhang Hua:	I hope so, too. Thank you for all you have done for me.
Jason:	You're very welcome.
Zhang Hua:	Don't forget to give us a call if you're in China. Take care of yourself.
Jason:	Take care. Bye! Have a good trip.

Li Hong:	We are just in time for the flight.
Elena:	Yes. It's very kind of you to see me off.
Li Hong:	My pleasure.
Elena:	Thank you very much for your hospitality during my stay here. I had a wonderful time.
Li Hong:	I'm glad you like our city. And we'll miss you. Keep in touch.
Elena:	Yes, I will.
Li Hong:	Give me a call when you arrive. Good-bye now.
Elena:	Good-bye.

II. Practice

1. Complete the following conversations and then act them out in pairs.

1) Li Min just met someone at a party, but he has to leave the party early.

Li Min:	Excuse me, but I'm afraid I won't be able to stay _____.
Lily:	But you've just come.
Li Min:	I'm very glad to have seen you and have had an enjoyable evening.
Lily:	It's _____ for us to see you go.
Li Min:	Goodbye. Take care of yourself and don't forget to _____.
Lily:	Sure. Good-bye.

2) Wang Lin is seeing someone off at the airport.

Steven:	Well, it's time to board the plane now!

Wang Lin: We're sorry _____.

Steven: Thank you for _____ you have done for me during my stay here.

Wang Lin: It's our pleasure. Hope we'll be able to get together again before long.

Steven: I really appreciate you coming to _____. Good-bye then.

Wang Lin: _____. Keep in touch.

2. Work in pairs. Practise saying good-bye with your partner according to the situations below. Then switch roles.

1) You have been invited to a birthday party and you are about to leave. You are saying good-bye to your host Tom Helmer.

2) You are visiting your friend in another city and you have to leave tomorrow. You are saying good-bye to your friend.

B) Listening

Listen to the eight conversations and choose the best answer to each question you hear.

1. A. 8:00.　　　　　　　B. 7:25.　　　　　　　C. 7:35.

2. A. She suggested he stay longer.

   B. She urged him to leave soon.

   C. She served him another drink.

3. A. By bike.　　　　　　B. On foot.　　　　　　C. By bus.

4. A. At the airport.　　　　B. At the train station.　　　C. At the bus stop.

5. A. He worked for a company.

   B. He paid a visit to a school.

   C. He studied in a university.

6. A. The day after tomorrow.　　B. Three days later.　　　C. Tomorrow.

7. A. She told David she would leave.

   B. She couldn't get through on the telephone.

   C. David failed to answer the call because he was out.

8. A. In the morning.　　　　B. In the afternoon.　　　C. In the evening.

Sounds and Spellings

I. Listen and practise. Pay special attention to the pronunciation of the italicized letters.

1. /f/　hal*f*, o*ff*er, tele*ph*one, lau*gh*
2. /v/　*v*ine, *v*egetable, Ste*ph*en
3. /θ/　au*th*or
4. /ð/　clo*th*es

II. Listen and practise. Pay special attention to the pronunciation of the plosives in continuous speech.

1. Good medicine for health tastes bitter to the mouth.　良药苦口利于病。
2. Adversity makes a man wise, not rich.　逆境出人才。
3. Virtue is fairer far than beauty.　美德远远胜过美貌。
4. All rivers run into the sea.　海纳百川。
5. There are two sides to every question.　问题皆有两面。

III. Read and enjoy.

November the Finest
November the finest
Five leaves left
One leaf falls
Four leaves left
☺☺☺☺☺

D Grammar

I. In each of the following sentences, there is a misused pronoun. Mark it out and then put the correct one in the brackets following each sentence.

1. Tom and me are responsible for this decision. (　　)
2. The boss has managed to put we workers in a bad situation. (　　)
3. Anyone here earns over a hundred dollars a day. (　　)
4. The student in that all-women's college should have no fear about their future. (　　)
5. Either the classrooms or the reading room must have their floor cleaned. (　　)
6. Nobody but her can solve this problem. (　　)
7. We enjoyed myself very much tonight. (　　)
8. This room is bigger than one next door. (　　)
9. Let's clean their room first and our later. (　　)
10. Last night, he and him friends went to a big bookstore. (　　)

II. Choose the one that best completes the sentence among the four choices marked A, B, C and D below each sentence.

1. Young people have more freedom in North America than in many _____ countries.
   A. the other   B. other   C. others   D. the others
2. When I arrived at the apartment, she told me to make _____ at home.
   A. herself   B. himself   C. myself   D. ourselves
3. You should take a small gift when you're invited to _____'s house for dinner.
   A. anyone   B. one   C. everyone   D. someone
4. The monkey's behavior differed from _____ of a healthy animal.
   A. this   B. that   C. these   D. those
5. I don't like this book. Give me a better _____.
   A. one   B. ones   C. book   D. books
6. _____ candidate is having an easy time with the press.
   A. Any   B. None   C. Either   D. Neither
7. Everybody must have _____ own choice.
   A. your   B. their   C. one's   D. our
8. I don't think we have met before. You are confusing me with _____.
   A. some other   B. one another   C. some one else   D. other person
9. Minerals are used by _____ of us in our daily lives.
   A. none   B. all   C. some   D. both

10. _____ crosses this line first will win the race.

    A. Whatever   B. Whomever   C. Whoever   D. Who

Writing

I. Writing for Specific Purposes

Text Messages

Text messages (also called SMS, shorten for Short Message Service) through cell phones became very popular in the late 1990s. It is becoming a preferred and cost-effective way of communicating with others.

In order to shorten the length, a text message should be very brief and to the point. Therefore, it has caused a whole new language to develop, and it uses abbreviations to express different words. For example, "r" for "are," "u" for "you," "2" for "to," "pls" for "please," "rks" for "rocks", etc. You'll find it saves you time when keying in a message and also makes Text Messaging a real fun and amusing way to communicate. To help you get started, we've written out a brief list which covers some frequently used abbreviations in text messages:

OIC—Oh I see.	Thx—Thanks
BRB—Be right back	Cya—See you
BFN—Bye for now	BCZ—Because
LOL—Laughing out loud	L8r—Later
FTF—Face to face	K—OK
ASAP—As soon as possible	D8—Date
BTW—By the way	Y—Why
FYI—For your information	U—You
JK—Just kidding	B4—Before
CWOT—Complete waste of time	2morro—Tomorrow
TTYL—Talk to you later	

II. Read the following text messages. Then rewrite them with complete words.

    1. CU LBR B4 U GO 2 WRK.

    2. My smmr hols wr CWOT. B4, we usd 2go2 NY 2C my bro, his GF & 3 kds FTF.

III. Write a text message to a friend.

    1. making an appointment to discuss the plan to spend the winter holidays;

    2. thanking him / her for a small gift.

TEXT B — Mother Goes to College

Sheri Straily never knew how far life's **highway** could take her — until her **dream** for her **children** helped her **find** out...

Growing up, Sheri never **thought** for a **moment** that she'd make it to college. Instead, she took a job **driving** a **truck**. As years **passed**, Sheri fell in love, **married** and had three children. Because she wanted to be **close** to home, she **switched** to a desk job at the trucking **company**.

But one day after work, as Sheri **watched** her **kids playing**, she began to think: I want them to **achieve** so much, but can I **afford** to give them the **opportunities** they'll need, like college?

Then it came to her: she was the one who needed college first!

"Go for it," her husband Steve **encouraged** her. So Sheri **enrolled** at the **University** of Denver's Women's College, which let her take all of her classes on **weekends** so she could still work.

Though Sheri loved her studies, she **missed** home: rather than make the two-hour **commute** to school, Sheri **stayed** in a **dorm** on weekends. I **wish** I were home with Steve and the kids, she'd think. But Eric, eight, Ryan, seven, and Kristin, five, **backed** their mom all the way. "Just do your best," they said.

Sheri did, getting **straight** A's as she **earned** a **degree** in **business administration**. Now she's **attending** the University of Denver **Law** School on a **merit scholarship**!

"It hasn't been easy," **notes** Sheri, "but it's **rewarding** — for me and my family."

(253 words)

New Words

highway	/ˈhaɪweɪ/	n.	公路;交通要道
dream	/driːm/	n.	梦想;睡梦　v. 做梦
child	/tʃaɪld/	n.	小孩,儿童
find	/faɪnd/	v.	找到,发现;感到

think	/θɪŋk/	v.	认为,以为
moment	/ˈməʊmənt/	n.	片刻;瞬间
drive	/draɪv/	v.	驾驶,行车
truck	/trʌk/	n.	载重货车;卡车
pass	/pɑːs/	v.	(时间)流逝;经过 　n. 通道;通行证
marry	/ˈmæri/	v.	结婚
close	/kləʊz/	a.	近的;亲密的　　v. 关闭;结束
switch	/swɪtʃ/	v.	转换,改变　　n. 转变;开关
company	/ˈkʌmpəni/	n.	公司;同伴
watch	/wɒtʃ/	v.	观看,注视;监视
kid	/kɪd/	n.	小孩;年轻人
play	/pleɪ/	v.	玩耍;扮演　　n. 游戏;戏剧
achieve	/əˈtʃiːv/	v.	达到;完成
afford	/əˈfɔːd/	v.	买得起,担负得起费用;提供
opportunity	/ˌɒpəˈtjuːnəti/	n.	机会,时机
encourage	/ɪnˈkʌrɪdʒ/	v.	鼓励,支持
▲enroll	/ɪnˈrəʊl/	v.	注册;加入;登记
★university	/ˌjuːnɪˈvɜːsəti/	n.	大学;高等学府
weekend	/ˌwiːkˈend/	n.	周末
miss	/mɪs/	v.	思念;未看到;未赶上
★commute	/kəˈmjuːt/	v.	每天上下班往返,定期往返
		n.	(上下班)两地之间定期往返
stay	/steɪ/	v.	停留,留下;保持
dorm	/dɔːm/	n.	寝室;(集体)宿舍
wish	/wɪʃ/	v.	希望(不大可能发生的事)发生;怀着(不大可能实现的)愿望
		n.	希望
back	/bæk/	v.	支持
straight	/streɪt/	a.	无间断的;整齐的;直的
earn	/ɜːn/	v.	获得;挣得;赚钱
degree	/dɪˈgriː/	n.	学位;程度,度数
business	/ˈbɪznəs/	n.	商业;生意;事务
administration	/ədˌmɪnɪˈstreɪʃn/	n.	管理,行政;管理部门
attend	/əˈtend/	v.	上(学);出席,参加;照料
law	/lɔː/	n.	法律
★merit	/ˈmerɪt/	n.	优点;美德
scholarship	/ˈskɒləʃɪp/	n.	奖学金;学识
note	/nəʊt/	v.	强调,着重提到;记下　　n. 笔记;注释
rewarding	/rɪˈwɔːdɪŋ/	a.	值得做的;有益的

Phrases and Expressions

find out	认识到,找出
for a moment	一会儿,片刻
fall in love	爱上
desk job	办公室工作
go for	努力获取
all the way	自始至终
do one's best	尽全力

Proper Names

Denver /ˈdenvə/ 丹佛(美国科罗拉多州首府)

课文词数	生词总量	生词比率	二级词汇	三级词汇	超纲词汇
253	40	15.8%	35	3	1

Judge , according to the text , whether the following statements are True or False.

1. _____ Sheri didn't know what her life goal was until her dream for her children had made her understand it.

2. _____ She worked in an office before she got married.

3. _____ Sheri chose the University of Denver's Women's College because she could take all courses at daytime.

4. _____ The family encouraged her to go to college.

5. _____ She was awarded a merit scholarship when she studied for the degree in business administration.

Being Mature

TEXT A   Am I Normal?

Since your last birthday, a lot of things have **changed**. For one, you're much **smarter** than you were last year. That's **obvious**. But there **might** have been some other changes. **Perhaps** you've **sprouted several inches** above everyone else in class. Or maybe they all did the sprouting and you **feel** too short. Now you're **looking** in the **mirror**, thinking only one thing: Am I normal?

Everybody's Different

First of all, what's normal? There's no one normal. **Otherwise**, the world would be full of a lot of **abnormal** people! The next time you go to the **mall**, take a look around. You'll see tall people, short people, and people with **broad shoulders**, little feet, big **stomachs**, long fingers, **stubby** legs, and **skinny** arms... you get the idea.

Small or Tall

Height is just one of the **thousands** of **features** your **genes decide**. In fact, because you have two parents, your genes act **like** a **referee**, giving you a height that usually **lands** somewhere between the height of each parent. If both your parents are tall, then most **likely** you will be tall, too.

But genes don't decide everything. For **example**, eating an **unhealthy diet** can keep you from growing to your **full potential**. Getting plenty of **sleep**, enough **exercise**, and **nutrients** will help you grow **just like** you should.

Weighing In

Weight can **vary** a lot, too, from kid to kid. Kids often weigh more or less than their friends and are still considered normal. TV and **magazines** might make us think our bodies

should weigh and look a certain way, but in real life, there are a lot of differences.

Some kids **worry** so much about their weight that they try unhealthy and dangerous things to change it. The best way to have a healthy weight is to eat right and get a lot of exercise.

(309 words)

New Words

normal	/ˈnɔːml/	a.	正常的;标准的
change	/tʃeɪndʒ/	v.	改变,兑换 _n._ 变化,零钱
smart	/smɑːt/	a.	漂亮的;聪明的
obvious	/ˈɔbviəs/	a.	显然的,明显的
might	/maɪt/	v.	可能,也许
perhaps	/pəˈhæps/	ad.	或许,可能
▲sprout	/spraʊt/	v.	(使)生长;发芽
several	/ˈsevrəl/	a.	几个,数个
inch	/ɪntʃ/	n.	英寸
feel	/fiːl/	v.	感觉;认为
look	/lʊk/	v.	看,瞧
mirror	/ˈmɪrə/	n.	镜子
otherwise	/ˈʌðəwaɪz/	ad.	否则,不然;除此之外 _conj._ 否则,不然
▲abnormal	/æbˈnɔːml/	a.	反常的;不正常的
mall	/mɔːl/	n.	购物中心,商场
broad	/brɔːd/	a.	宽的;广泛的
shoulder	/ˈʃəʊldə/	n.	肩(部)
stomach	/ˈstʌmək/	n.	胃,肚子
▲stubby	/ˈstʌbi/	a.	粗短的,矮胖的
▲skinny	/ˈskɪni/	n.	皮包骨的,瘦削的
height	/haɪt/	n.	高度,身高
thousand	/ˈθaʊznd/	num.	千;(pl.)成千上万
feature	/ˈfiːtʃə/	n.	特色;(pl.)相貌
★gene	/dʒiːn/	n.	遗传基因
decide	/dɪˈsaɪd/	v.	决定;裁决
like	/laɪk/	prep.	像……一样,如

▲referee	/ˌrefəˈriː/	n.	证明人；裁判员
usually	/ˈjuːʒuəli/	ad.	通常
land	/lænd/	v.	陷入，落入，处于某种状态；(使)登陆，(使)着陆
likely	/ˈlaɪkli/	ad.	很可能
		a.	可能的；有希望的
example	/ɪɡˈzɑːmpl/	n.	实例；范例
unhealthy	/ʌnˈhelθi/	a.	不健康的，不健壮的
diet	/ˈdaɪət/	n.	日常饮食；规定饮食
full	/fʊl/	a.	(充)满的；完全的
★potential	/pəˈtenʃl/	n.	潜能，潜力　　a.潜在的，可能的
sleep	/ˈsliːp/	v.	睡，睡觉　　n.睡，睡觉
exercise	/ˈeksəsaɪz/	n.	锻炼；练习　　v.锻炼；运用
▲nutrient	/ˈnjuːtriənt/	n.	营养品；营养素
just	/dʒʌst/	ad.	正好，恰恰正是；刚才
★weigh	/weɪ/	v.	称(…的重量)；权衡
★weight	/weɪt/	n.	重量，体重
★vary	/ˈveəri/	v.	改变，(使)变化
magazine	/ˌmægəˈziːn/	n.	杂志，期刊
worry	/ˈwʌri/	v.	(使)担心，(使)发愁　　n.担心，忧虑

Phrases and Expressions

be full of	有很多，充满
in fact	事实上；实际上
act like	担任；充当…的作用
keep sb. from doing sth.	使…不做某事
plenty of	许多
vary from… to…	由…到…情况不等
in real life	在现实生活中
worry about	担心，担忧

课文词数	生词总量	生词比率	二级词汇	三级词汇	超纲词汇
309	44	14.2%	33	5	6

GETTING THE MESSAGE

I. Recite the third and the fourth paragraphs of the text.

II. Decide which of the following best states the main idea of the passage.

A. Genes decide your features exclusively.

B. Both genes and healthy living habits play an important role for people to be "normal" in height and weight.

C. There are a lot of abnormal people in the world with broad shoulders, little feet, big stomachs, long fingers, stubby legs, and skinny arms.

D. It is advisable to try unhealthy and dangerous things to lose weight.

III. Answer the following questions.

1. While growing up, how will the kids usually change each year?

2. According to the text, is it true that if both your parents are tall, then most likely you will also be tall? Illustrate your point of view with examples, please.

3. What are the main factors that influence one's normal growth?

4. According to the author, what is the best way to have a healthy weight? What is your opinon?

VOCABULARY AND STRUCTURE

I. Match words or phrases in Column A with their explanations in Column B.

A	B
1. sprout	a. enough or more than enough, or a large amount
2. plenty	b. the kind of food that a person or animal eats each day
3. potential	c. very different from usual in a way that seems strange
4. mall	d. short and thick or fat
5. skinny	e. (vegetables, seeds, or plants) start to grow, or producing shoots, buds or leaves
6. stubby	f. shopping center
7. abnormal	g. possible; possibility
8. diet	h. any substance which plants or animals need in order to live and grow
9. smart	i. very thin
10. nutrient	j. intelligent or sensible

II. Fill in the blanks in each sentence with a word or phrase taken from the box below. Change the word form if necessary.

vary   normal   feature   smart   worry about   referee   obvious   decide

1. Richard only lost the game because the _____ was biased.

2. My daughter's taste in classical music _____ widely, but she usually prefers Mozart or Brahms.

3. A meeting was called to _____ between the three candidates. After a long discussion, they were in favour of the foreigner.

4. The hotel's distinguishing _____ are that it is cheap and convenient.

5. The temperature was below _____ for the time of year.

6. You've really got no need to _____ your weight.

III. Rewrite the following sentences after the model.

Model

Children who live in the rural areas *are* very *likely to* be poor.
It is *likely that* children who live in the rural areas are poor.

1. Young drivers are *likely to* have more accidents than older ones.

_____.

2. Everybody is *likely to* have a successful life career with vision, determination, self-respect, and hard work.

_____.

For example, eating an unhealthy diet can *keep* you *from* growing to your full potential.
For example, eating an unhealthy diet can *prevent* you *from* growing to your full potential.

1. Her ex-husband had *kept her from seeing* her children.

_____.

2. His leg injury may *keep him from playing* in tomorrow's football game.

_____.

IV. Translate the following sentences into Chinese.

1. But in real life, there are a lot of differences.

2. Height is just one of the thousands of features your genes decide.

3. But genes don't decide everything. For example, eating an unhealthy diet can keep you from growing to your full potential.

V. Translate the following sentences with words or phrases learnt in Text A.

1. 这部电影太乏味了,我几乎忍不住睡着了。(keep… from)

2. 盆子里装了满满的一盆热水。(be full of)

3. 史密斯夫妇决定去澳洲度寒假。(decide to do)

4. 我的老师认为女孩对足球感兴趣是不寻常的。(abnormal)

5. 改变你的饮食习惯是减肥的最佳方法。(change)

 **Speaking**

I. Expressing Thanks

☺ Expressing thanks is universally held as being civilized. It is quite proper to say "Thank you" when we recognize that someone has done something for us, no matter how small it is and no matter whether he is a superior or a servant. Thus we thank people for an invitation, an offer or help, a present, etc.

☺ Differences arise between the Chinese and the English-speaking people in that traditional Chinese customs don't require people to express thanks for small favors, while "Thank you" is very common in English-speaking countries, even between parents and children, husband and wife and for very small and most ordinary things.

☺ Additionally, Chinese and Western cultures have different responses to expressions of gratitude. For instance, "It doesn't matter" or "Never mind" are responses to apologies, not to thanks. And "This is what I should do" or "It's my duty to do so" are not responses to thanks in English, for a native English speaker may find it inappropriate to respond with "It's my duty to do so", which suggests "You don't have to thank me. I had no choice but to do it, because it is my duty, otherwise I would not have done so." This is, of course, far from the message the Chinese intends to convey.

Useful Sentences

Thank you ever so much.	You are welcome.
Thank you just the same.	Not at all.
I appreciate it.	I'm glad you like it.
I want to express my appreciation to all my friends for their support.	It's a pleasure./You are welcome./Don't mention it/I'm happy I could do that.
I'm very grateful to you.	Don't mention it.
I'm thankful to you for all the beautiful gifts.	It's my pleasure. /I'm so glad if it gives you pleasure.
Thank you very much again.	It's nothing at all.
Words can't express how honored I feel at the moment.	You are welcome.
Thank you for the enjoyable evening.	It is a pleasure to have you.

Model 1

Mary: Hello, Jack!

Jack: Hi, Mary. How are you feeling now?

Mary: Oh, much better. Thank you. And thank you very much for the bouquet of flowers.

Jack: I'm glad you like them. You know they are from my own garden.

Mary: They are so beautiful and lovely!

Jack: I know you love flowers, and I hope you enjoy them.

Mary: Surely. You are always so kind and thoughtful.

Model 2

Bill: Congratulations, John! I've got the good news you were named Excellent Student.

John: Thank you. Mr. Black.

Bill: I really feel happy for you. I know you deserve the honor.

John: It's very kind of you to say so.

Bill: I've talked with other teachers about you, and I was very much impressed.

John: I owe much to your kind help and support, Mr. Black.

Bill: Well, I'm sure you will be more successful in your study next term.

John: Thanks for your kind words. I'm looking forward to my greater progress in the future with your help.

II. Practice

1. Match the following expressions of thanks in column A with proper responses in column B.

A	B
1) Thanks, Dana, for helping me with my heavy luggage.	A. I am so glad if it gives you pleasure.
2) Thank you for your gift for me. I like it very much.	B. I'm so glad that you could come. I do hope you will be able to come again very soon.
3) I'm afraid I have to go now, Mrs. Martin. Thanks for the wonderful evening.	C. You're entirely welcome.
4) Thank you so much for your suggestions. I'm really grateful to you.	D. Don't mention it. It was the least I could do.
5) Thank you for your direction in ordering our meal.	E. It's my pleasure. I hope you will enjoy it very much.
6) I don't know what I'd have done without your help.	F. Oh, it's no trouble at all. I'm glad that I can help you.

2. Work in pairs. Imagine you have finished your term paper and you've just received the corrected copy with some suggestions from Professor Smith. You meet him on campus and express your thanks. Make a conversation with your partner, and then perform it in front of your classmates. Practice greeting with your partner according to the situations above. Then switch roles.

B Listening

Listen to the eight conversations and choose the best answer to each question you hear.

1. A. Orange juice   B. Coffee   C. Tea

2. A. The woman didn't invite the man.

  B. The woman invited the man.

  C. The man didn't want to go to the party.

3. A. She will take a seat.

  B. She will ask for a seat.

  C. She will think for a moment.

4. A. In a school.   B. In a factory.   C. In a clinic.

5. A. America.   B. Canada.   C. Britain.

6. A. Because the woman studies well.

  B. Because Tom wants to ask the woman for help.

  C. Because the woman helped Tom with his study.

7. A. She will send flowers to her mother.

  B. She will thank the man for his flowers.

  C. She will visit her mother tomorrow.

8. A. The woman wanted the man to help her again.

  B. The woman thanked the man for his help.

  C. The man likes to help people.

C Sounds and Spellings

I. Listen and practise. Pay special attention to the pronunciation of the italicized letters.

1. /s/	hou*s*e, *s*quare, *c*entury, gla*ss*, ex*c*use, *c*ycle, de*c*ide
2. /z/	ro*s*e, the*s*e, *z*ip, do*s*e, alway*s*, ha*s*
3. /ʃ/	*sh*ine, *sh*are, wa*sh*, *sh*ell, sea*sh*ore, *s*ure
4. /ʒ/	plea*s*ure, trea*s*ure, mea*s*ure, gara*g*e
5. /h/	*h*eight, *h*air, *h*appy, *h*ope, *h*uman

II. Listen and practise. Pay special attention to the pronunciation of the plosives in continuous speech.

| 1. Harp not for ever on the same string.　勿老调重弹。 |
| 2. He that promises too much means nothing.　轻诺必寡信。 |
| 3. From saving comes having.　富有来自节俭。 |
| 4. The fire is the test of gold; adversity of strong man.烈火试真金,困苦炼壮士。 |
| 5. Where there is life, there is hope.　生命不息,希望长在。 |

III. Read and enjoy.

1. Sure the ship's shipshape, sir.
2. We surely shall see the sun shine soon.
3. She sells sea shells on the sea shore;
   The shells that she sells are sea shells I'm sure.
   So if she sells sea shells on the sea shore,
   I'm sure that the shells are sea shore shells.

☺☺☺☺☺

D Grammar

I. Fill in the blanks with the words given and change the form of words when necessary.

1. There are _____ books in the library I'd like to read. (thousands of, thousand of)

2. The number of giant pandas is getting _____ because their living areas are becoming farmlands. (smaller and smaller, fewer and fewer)

3. They arrived in _____. (two and three, twos and threes)

4. Five hundred Yuan a month _____ enough to live on. (are, is)

5. _____ of the buildings in this coastal area were ruined in the heavy storm. (Three-fourths, Three fourth)

6. She is industrious and became a professor in her _____. (early thirty, early thirties)

7. We've tried it three times. Must we try it _____? (a fourth time, four time)

8. It's _____ distance from our campus to the Bell Tower. (three kilometer's, three kilometers')

9. Please turn to _____. Let's read the text aloud. (Page Two, the page two)

10. During _____ century, the world population reached 6 billion. (the twentieth, Twentieth)

II. Choose the one that best completes the sentence among the four choices marked A, B, C and D below each sentence.

1. My new bicycle cost me about _____ my old one.
   A. three times than   B. three times as much as
   C. three times much than   D. three times as many as

2. The assignment for this weekend is to write an _____ essay on the influence of globalization on education and culture.
   A. eight-hundred-word   B. eight-hundred-words
   C. eight-hundreds-words   D. eight-hundreds-word

3. _____ of the students in our class are from the south.
   A. Four-ninth   B. Fours-ninth   C. Four-ninths   D. Fours-ninths

4. "When will you leave for Australia?"
   "On Sunday, _____."
   A. sixth January   B. the sixth of January
   C. the six January   D. the six of January

5. The weight of the moon is only about _____ of the earth.

A. one eighty　　　　　　　　B. one of eighty

C. one the eighties　　　　　　D. one eightieth

6. As he is poor in health, he goes to his factory only _____ just to learn something about the progress of the experiment.

A. once a week　　　　　　　B. one week

C. one time a week　　　　　　D. one a week

7. The population of many big cities in China has _____ in the past ten years.

A. more than doubled　　　　　B. more doubled than

C. much than doubled　　　　　D. much doubled than

8. As is known, the Olympic Games are held _____.

A. every four years　　　　　　B. every four year

C. every fourth years　　　　　D. every four-years

9. Three students _____ in this university come from Chengdu.

A. of ten　　　　B. out of in ten　　　　C. out of ten　　　　D. in tens

10. The games of _____ Olympics will be held in Beijing this summer.

A. 29　　　　B. the 29th　　　　C. the 29　　　　D. 29th

Writing

I. Write a thank-you note to your host family with whom you spent Christmas Day in Australia according to the dialogue.

A: I'm leaving for China tomorrow. I just can't go without saying thanks to you.

B: Oh, I hate to say good-bye to you. It's nice to have had you with our family.

A: I'll never forget the days we spent and enjoyed together. You've done so much for me.

B: It's my pleasure. I'll miss you. Please keep in touch.

II. Writing for specific purposes

Here is an example of a postcard template. Read the sample postcard and write a postcard to your friend, telling him or her about your last holiday in Sydney, including the following information:

the weather; something you did yesterday; the family you stay with; something you are going to do today

Tips for Writing

A Post Card

A post card is usually brief, friendly and informal. Especially, it's a popular form of holiday correspondence.

- A post card has limited writing space as there is usually a picture on one side and the address of the recipient is written on half of the other side.
- Only concise, relevant information should, therefore, be included.
- Date and place need to be specified.
- Fragment language with phrases and incomplete sentences are allowable.
- Include as many interesting details as possible.
- The tone will vary according to the relationship between sender and recipient.

Sample

12 July

Dear Mum and Dad,

I arrived in Beijing yesterday by plane. We are staying in a hotel near the Tian An Men Square. Yesterday, we visited the Great Wall, and I was awarded a prize for successfully climbing to the top. Tomorrow we shall visit Beijing University.

Best wishes!

Jenny

Mrs. Joan Hunt
704 Lincon Drive
New York
NY122123
USA

Airmail

TEXT B   How to Be a Young Adult

You're **hitting** the end of those **teen** years, and are **quickly approaching** your 20s. Since you are now **officially** a young adult, here's how to start **acting** like one.

1. If you **screw up**, don't **lie** about it or pass on the **blame** to someone else. **Admit** your mistake, **apologize**, and ask what you can do to **correct** the **situation** or make things right.

2. **Get** a job or work **towards** getting one. Have a plan so your parents don't support you **indefinitely**.

3. When you get a job, be **grateful** for it, work hard, **follow** the **rules** of the company. Don't **whine** or **complain** about your **duties**, **treatment**, or **pay**.

4. Watch the **news** on a large news **outlet**. Know a little about politics and **current events**.

5. Read your **local** newspaper — and not just the **sports** or **lifestyle section**.

6. **Accept** the fact that most adults actually might know what they are talking about — and you can even learn something from the ones who don't.

7. Make friends with **responsible** adults who are older than you. Ask for their advice on things and listen to the **advice** you're given.

8. Think about where you want your life to be in five years. **Make** a **plan** about how you will get there.

9. Avoid **alcohol**. "**Mature**" is not the first **adjective** that most people will think of if they see you **drunk**.

10. Putting part of your **paycheck** into your savings account is going to be useful when you want a house or car.

11. Make your payments on time, and it will be easier to get approval for large purchases in a few years.

12. Know that you cannot control other people so try not to think too much or care about what others think of you.

13. Respect your parents. They are the people who will be there most likely when you need help.

(317 words)

New Words

young	/jʌŋ/	a.	幼小的;年轻的
hit	/hɪt/	v.	到达;击,打
▲teen	/tiːn/	a.	青少年的
quickly	/ˈkwɪkli/	ad.	迅速地,很快地
approach	/əˈprəʊtʃ/	v.	接近,靠近　　　n. 接近;方式
officially	/əˈfɪʃəli/	ad.	正式地,官方地
act	/ækt/	v.	行动;起作用;表演　　n. 行为,动作
★screw	/skruː/	n.	螺丝,螺丝(钉)　　v. 拧,拧紧
up	/ʌp/	ad.	向上,往上　　prep. 向上,在上
lie	/laɪ/	v.	说谎;躺　　n. 谎言,假话
blame	/bleɪm/	n.	责怪;责备　　v. 把…归咎于
admit	/ədˈmɪt/	v.	承认
apologize	/əˈpɒlədʒaɪz/	v.	道歉
correct	/kəˈrekt/	v.	改正,纠正　　a. 正确的
situation	/ˌsɪtʃuˈeɪʃn/	n.	情况,状况
get	/get/	v.	接到,得到
towards	/təˈwɔːdz/	prep.	向,朝
▲indefinitely	/ɪnˈdefɪnətli/	ad.	无限期地
grateful	/ˈgreɪtfl/	a.	感激的,感谢的
follow	/ˈfɒləʊ/	v.	跟随;遵守
rule	/ruːl/	n.	规则,常规
▲whine	/waɪn/	v.	哀诉;啼哭
		n.	长而高音的响声(尤指烦人的,狗或儿童发出的)
complain	/kəmˈpleɪn/	v.	抱怨,埋怨
duty	/ˈdjuːti/	n.	责任,义务
treatment	/ˈtriːtmənt/	n.	治疗,对待
pay	/peɪ/	n.	工资,薪水
news	/njuːz/	n.	消息,新闻
★outlet	/ˈaʊtlet/	n.	经销店,出路
current	/ˈkʌrənt/	a.	当前的,现在的
		n.	(空气,水等的)流,流速;电流
event	/ɪˈvent/	n.	大事,重要事情

local	/ˈləʊkl/	a.	地方的,当地的
sport	/ˈspɔːt/	n.	体育运动
▲lifestyle	/ˈlaɪfstaɪl/	n.	生活方式
section	/ˈsekʃn/	n.	(报纸的)栏;部分;部门
accept	/əkˈsept/	v.	接受;同意,认可
responsible	/rɪˈspɒntsəbl/	a.	有责任感的,负责的
advice	/ədˈvaɪs/	v.	忠告,建议
make	/meɪk/	v.	制造,做
plan	/plæn/	n.	计划,方案　　v. 计划,安排
alcohol	/ˈælkəhɒl/	n.	酒,酒精
mature	/məˈtʃʊə/	a.	成熟的　　v. (使)成熟
adjective	/ˈædʒɪktɪv/	n.	形容词
drunk	/drʌŋk/	adj.	(酒)醉的,陶醉的
▲paycheck	/peɪtʃek/	n.	薪水;付薪水的支票

Phrases and Expressions

screw up	(俚)搞糟,毁坏
be grateful to (sb.) for (sth.)	感激…,对…感谢
complain about	抱怨
savings account	存折
care about	关心

课文词数	生词总量	生词比率	二级词汇	三级词汇	超纲词汇
317	44	13.9%	37	2	5

Judge, according to the text, whether the following statements are True or False.

1. _____ It is acceptable for young people in their 20s to ignore his or her mistakes.

2. _____ If you are drunk, people don't think that you are mature.

3. _____ It is unnecessary for young people to put some money aside to buy a house or a car.

4. _____ Try to pay your money as scheduled, or it is not easy for you to get credit.

5. _____ Parents are always with you when you are in trouble.

Ways to Success

TEXT A The Way to Success

Everyone **craves** for success, but how to approach it is a **complicated** problem. There are surely many factors **related** to this matter, among which are **diligence**, **confidence**, **optimism**, **cooperation** with others and so forth.

Diligence, in my opinion, is the first and **foremost** element for achievements. An **industrious** person can **accumulate** more and more experience which counts much with his later success. On the contrary, a man who keeps talking big but never puts his plan into action would **eventually** amount to nothing, however **ambitious** he should be.

Confidence, to some **extent**, is also of great **importance contributing** to a **brilliant** career. Any **favorable** chance can easily **slip** away while one **hesitates** for lack of self-confidence. A self-confident man, in general, **tends** to catch one opportunity after another, which may at last lead him to success.

Optimism, in any case, is an **essential component** directing to one's **prosperity**. It's almost **inevitable** to **encounter failure** some time or other. An **optimist** is **inclined** to stand up against such **misfortune** and **draw** useful lessons from them to avoid more serious ones. If you are a loser and give up **trials** forever, then you are definitely **denied access** to any success.

Cooperation with others, for my part, is the last but not the least **consideration** of great **feats**. Hardly anytime can you **imagine** a **purposeful** man without any aid from others could **fulfill** his task **perfectly**; especially in modern society where projects become more complex than ever, people need to work together **effectively**. **Furthermore**, as a

proverb goes, "Two heads are better than one." People in cooperation are likely to put forward better ideas suitable to **solve** the very problem.

In order to be successful, one has to be as diligent, confident, **optimistic** and **cooperative** as stated above. These factors are related as **necessities** to succeed. Everyone has to act upon these **aspects** on the **arduous** way to turn their efforts into reality.

(320 words)

New Words

success	/sək'ses/	n.	成功,胜利;成功的人或物
▲crave	/kreɪv/	v.	渴望;恳求
★complicated	/'kɒmplɪkeɪtɪd/	a.	复杂的,难懂的
related	/rɪ'leɪtɪd/	a.	有关的,相关的
▲diligence	/'dɪlɪdʒəns/	n.	勤奋;认真刻苦
confidence	/'kɒnfɪdəns/	n.	自信,信心;信任
optimism	/'ɒptɪmɪzəm/	n.	乐观;乐观主义
★cooperation	/kəʊˌɒpə'reɪʃn/	n.	合作,协作
▲foremost	/'fɔːməʊst/	a.	最重要的;最著名的
▲industrious	/ɪn'dʌstriəs/	a.	勤奋的;勤劳的
★accumulate	/ə'kjuːmjʊleɪt/	v.	积累;增加
★eventually	/ɪ'ventʃʊəli/	ad.	最后,终于
★ambitious	/æm'bɪʃəs/	a.	有雄心的, 有壮志的
extent	/ɪk'stent/	n.	程度
importance	/ɪm'pɔːtns/	n.	重要性, 有价值
contribute	/kən'trɪbjuːt/	v.	有助于, 促成;贡献, 捐献
brilliant	/'brɪliənt/	a.	杰出的;非常明亮的
favorable	/'feɪvərəbl/	a.	合适的,有利的;赞成的
slip	/slɪp/	v.	溜走;滑动
hesitate	/'hezɪteɪt/	v.	迟疑, 犹豫不决
★tend	/tend/	v.	倾向;朝某方向
★essential	/ɪ'senʃl/	a.	必要的, 不可缺少的;本质的

★component	/kəmˈpəʊnənt/	n.	组成部分;零部件
★prosperity	/prɒˈsperəti/	n.	成功;(经济上的) 繁荣
★inevitable	/ɪnˈevɪtəbl/	a.	不可避免的
★encounter	/ɪnˈkaʊntə/	v.	遇到,遭遇;与…邂逅
failure	/ˈfeɪljə/	n.	失败
optimist	/ˈɒptɪmɪst/	n.	乐观主义者
★incline	/ɪnˈklaɪn/	v.	倾向于,易于;向某方向倾斜
misfortune	/ˌmɪsˈfɔːtʃuːn/	n.	不幸,厄运;灾难
draw	/drɔː/	v.	汲取,获取;画图
trial	/ˈtraɪəl/	n.	尝试;审判
deny	/dɪˈnaɪ/	v.	阻止某人获得;否认,不承认
★access	/ˈækses/	n.	接近,进入;方法,通路,机会
consideration	/kənˌsɪdəˈreɪʃn/	n.	因素;考虑
▲feat	/fiːt/	n.	伟业,功绩
imagine	/ɪˈmædʒɪn/	v.	想象,认为
purposeful	/ˈpɜːpəsfl/	a.	坚定的,有毅力的
fulfill	/fʊlˈfɪl/	v.	完成,实现;满足
perfectly	/ˈpɜːfɪktli/	ad.	完美地;完全地
effectively	/ɪˈfektɪvli/	ad.	有效地;实际上地
furthermore	/ˌfɜːðəˈmɔː/	ad.	而且,此外
▲proverb	/ˈprɒvɜːb/	n.	格言,谚语
solve	/sɒlv/	v.	解决
optimistic	/ˌɒptɪˈmɪstɪk/	a.	乐观的,有信心的
★cooperative	/kəʊˈɒpərətɪv/	a.	合作的,协作的;联营的
necessity	/nɪˈsesəti/	n.	需要,必要性;必需品
aspect	/ˈæspekt/	n.	方面;方向,方位
▲arduous	/ˈɑːdjʊəs/	a.	艰苦的,艰巨的;费力的

Phrases and Expressions

crave for	渴望得到
and so forth	诸如此类,等等
in one's opinion	依照某人的看法
on the contrary	正好相反
to some extent	某种程度上说

Unit 4
Ways to Success

in general	一般来说，大体上
in any case	无论如何，不管怎样
stand up against	直面，正确对待
be likely to	很有可能
put forward	提出

课文词数	生词总量	生词比率	二级词汇	三级词汇	超纲词汇
320	49	15.3%	28	14	7

GETTING THE MESSAGE

I. Fill in the blanks without referring to the original text. After that, check your answers against the original.

In order to be _____, one has to be as diligent, _____, optimistic and cooperative as stated _____. These factors are related as necessities to succeed. _____ has to act upon these aspects on the arduous _____ to turn his or her efforts into _____.

II. Decide which of the following best states the main idea of the passage.

A. How to approach success is a complicated problem.

B. Diligence, confidence, optimism and cooperation with others are the essential factors which lead to success.

C. Those who are diligent, confident, optimistic and cooperative tend to catch more opportunities.

D. In order to succeed, everyone has to turn their efforts into reality.

III. Answer the following questions.

1. In the author's opinion, what is the most essential element to success?

2. When will a favorable chance easily slip away?

3. What does "Two heads are better than one." mean?

4. Do you think you can fulfill your task perfectly without cooperation with others? Why?

══ **VOCABULARY AND STRUCTURE** ══

I. Match words in Column A with their explanations in Column B.

A	B
1. diligence	a. to have a strong desire for sth.
2. cooperation	b. steady effort, careful hard work
3. crave	c. feeling of certainty
4. draw	d. acting or working together for a common purpose
5. confidence	e. necessary or most important
6. essential	f. to help to cause sth.
7. purposeful	g. outstanding
8. contribute	h. suitable or helpful
9. brilliant	i. having or showing determination or will-power
10. favourable	j. to gain or derive from study or experience

II. Fill in the blank in each sentence with a word or phrase taken from the box below. Change the word form if necessary.

slip away	tend to	to some extent	aspect
put forward	favorable	on the contrary	consideration

1. _____, these aspects reflect modern Chinese anxiety.

2. He _____ a plan for the committee to consider.

3. I'm not sick; _____, I'm in the peak of health.

4. She _____ before the end of the meeting.

5. Plants _____ die in hot weather if you don't water them.

6. We must consider a problem in all its _____.

III. Rewrite the following sentences after the model.

 **Model**

You should keep on doing exercises every day, *however* healthy you are.
No matter how healthy you are, you should keep on doing exercises every day.

1. He couldn't get a promotion, *however* hard he tried.

   _____.

2. I will carry it out, *however* difficult the task may be.

   _____.

Science is *of great help* to the development of the cinema.
Science is *very helpful* to the development of the cinema.

3. This kind of tool is *of great use*.

   _____.

4. The chance is *of great importance* to every one of us.

   _____.

IV. Translate the following sentences into Chinese.

1. Everyone craves for success, but how to approach it is a complicated problem.

2. Any favorable chance can easily slip away while one hesitates for lack of self-confidence.

3. If you are a loser and give up trials forever, then you are definitely denied access to any success.

V. Translate the following sentences with words or phrases learnt in Text A.

1. 中国人对 2008 年奥运会取得成功充满信心。(confidence)

2. 在她看来,这些历史书籍似乎很重,她一个人搬不动。(in one's opinion)

3. 一般来说,春天是一个几乎每个人都喜欢的季节。(in general)

4. 我们当中没有一个人可能去坐李教授旁边的那个座位。(be likely to)

5. 无论如何我会先把票订好。(in any case)

 Speaking

I. How to Make Apologies

Some "Do's" in Apologizing to People

☺ In daily life, everyone makes mistakes and everyone needs to know what to say and what to do after making a mistake. When you do something wrong or fail to do something necessary, you can save a lot of trouble by apologizing first before someone complains to you. When you apologize, sometimes you need to offer an excuse or reason. The excuse is normally given immediately after the apology. It is important to make your apology genuine and sincere and to keep your promise as best as you can. Use the appropriate facial expression or gesture to show that you are truly sorry.

Useful Sentence Patterns	
I'm sorry about…	That's (quite) all right.
I really feel bad about…	(Oh, well.) Not to worry.
I'm sorry I couldn't…	These things happen. It can't be helped.
I apologize for…	Never mind. It's nothing unusual.
I'm afraid I seem to have…	Oh, that's all right. Don't be upset about it.
I owe you an apology for…	I can understand. Please don't worry.
Please accept my apologies for not…	It doesn't matter.
I'm terribly sorry about…	No problem. Let's forget it.
I beg your pardon for…	No, don't bother. We all make mistakes.
Excuse me for…	Don't take it to heart.
I hope you excuse me.	

Please forgive me.	
I'm sorry. I didn't mean to…	
How silly of me to…	

Model

Mum: You're late for supper, Bill.

Son: I'm terribly sorry about it, Mum.

Mum: That's all right. What's the matter?

Son: I have to work overtime to finish my course paper these days.

Mum: Hmm. It's not your fault. But why not do it at home?

Son: I have to have a discussion with my classmates.

Mum: I see. Remember to call next time.

Son: All right. I'll do that.

Tom: Please forgive me, Jimmy.

Jimmy: Forgive you? What for?

Tom: I unplugged your computer before I realized it was still in use.

Jimmy: No. You are kidding!

Tom: You were out and I didn't notice that. I really feel bad about it.

Jimmy: Oh, my God! When can I finish typing my course paper?

Tom: It's my fault. What can I do to make it up to you?

Jimmy: I accept your apologies. I'll type it again.

Tom: Let me help you type.

Jimmy: It doesn't matter. I'll do it myself.

II. Practice

1. Complete the following conversation and then act it out in pairs.

James: Why do you look so upset? _____?

Kathy: Where were you yesterday? I kept _____ on your
cell phone all afternoon. But when I called, I only heard "The power is off".
_____ you had to do that?

James: Uh, I was attending _____ given by a well-known professor, so I had to _____. No wonder you couldn't reach me.

Kathy: I see. You know what yesterday was? It was _____

_____.

James: Oh, _____ to have forgotten your birthday! I hope you _____.

Kathy: That's all right. I can understand.

James: I'll _____ it.

Kathy: No problem. Let's forget it.

James: Really, _____ about that.

Kathy: Have you ever heard _____ "Love means never having to say you're sorry"?

James: Aha! Ok, Ok.

2. Work in pairs. Practice making an apology to your partner according to the situation below. Then switch roles.

One day Student A broke a new MP4 player of Student B's. He makes an apology for it.

B **Listening**

Listen to the four conversations and choose the best answer to each question you hear.

1. A. Accounting.   B. Marketing.   C. Computer science.

2. A. On East Campus.   B. On West Campus.   C. On South Campus.

3. A. He turned off his alarm clock and went back to sleep again.

   B. His mother didn't wake him up on time.

   C. He got on the wrong bus and lost his way.

4. A. In his schoolbag.   B. At home.   C. In his teacher's office.

5. A. Because he smokes in front of the woman.

   B. Because he shouts at the woman.

   C. Because he made a little mistake.

6. A. Uncomfortable.   B. Understanding.   C. Indifferent.

7. A. A library.   B. A post office.   C. A subway station.

8. A. It's opposite the subway station.   B. It's in front of the subway station.

 C. It's behind the subway station.

 ## Sounds and Spellings

I. Listen and practise. Pay special attention to the pronunciation of the italicized letters.

1. /tʃ/   *ch*ild
2. /dʒ/   *j*oin, ju*dg*e, stran*ge*
3. /m/   fa*m*e
4. /n/   thi*n*, begi*nn*ing
5. /ŋ/   bri*ng*, thi*n*k, nothi*ng*

II. Listen and practise. Pay special attention to the pronunciation of the plosives in continuous speech.

1. No man can do two things at once.   一心不可二用。
2. A fox may grow gray, but never good.   江山易改,本性难移。
3. A good beginning is half done.   良好的开端是成功的一半。
4. A good fame is better than a good face.   美名胜过美貌。
5. A good medicine tastes bitter.   良药苦口。

III. Read and enjoy.

> A man goes to church and starts talking to God. He says: "God, what is a million dollars to you?" and God says: "A penny", then the man says: "God, what is a million years to you?" and God says: "a second", then the man says: "God, can I have a penny?" and God says: "In a second."
>
> ☺☺☺☺☺

D Grammar

I. Fill in the blanks with definite and indefinite articles (a / an / the) when necessary.

1. _____ sun is like a great ball of fire in _____ sky.
2. I bought _____ umbrella at _____ small store nearby.
3. On _____ Saturday evening, we usually have a good time.
4. Most of _____ students in our college are fond of _____ sports.
5. Betty is _____ honest girl and she studies _____ hardest in her class.
6. He was elected _____ chairman of _____ Olympic Committee.
7. I bought _____ useful dictionary, which helps me enlarge my vocabulary.
8. My brother is fond of playing _____ football while my sister likes playing _____ piano.
9. _____ wounded were taken to _____ hospital immediately.
10. When did _____ First World War break out?

II. Choose the one that best completes the sentence among the four choices marked A, B, C and D below each sentence.

1. The two girls are such good friends that they frequently exchange gifts with _____.
   A. each other   B. the other   C. another   D. the others
2. Plant the trees on _____ side of the street.
   A. both   B. any   C. every   D. either
3. Do you remember _____ he said at the meeting.
   A. all what   B. all which   C. all that   D. that
4. _____ in our country has a right to education.
   A. Everyone   B. All   C. Someone   D. No one
5. Without careful investigation, _____ is likely to come to wrong conclusions.
   A. each   B. any one   C. someone   D. no one
6. The speed of radio waves is equal to _____.
   A. light   B. this of light   C. those of light   D. that of light
7. Disappointed by the result of the experiment, she started _____.
   A. it   B. them   C. a new one   D. new the one
8. A lot of young men have tried, but _____ have succeeded.
   A. some   B. few   C. a few   D. many
9. I agree with most of what you said, but I don't agree with _____.

A. nothing   B. something   C. anything   D. everything

10. It is a pity that we should stay at home when we have _____.

A. such fine weather   B. such a fine weather

C. so fine weather   D. so fine a weather

Writing

General Writing

Read the following paragraph and then write a short paragraph of your own which states your views on success.

I think people will become successful if they work hard at what they want to achieve. They do not give up even if they don't get something right at the first time. They usually keep practising until they get the desired results. They are always moving toward their goals. To me, successful people are not necessarily famous ones. There are successful people in your office or in your neighborhood.

TEXT B   The Role of Luck in Success

"When people **succeed**, it is because of hard work. Luck has nothing to do with success." Do you agree or **disagree** with the **quotation** above?

It has been said that when people succeed, it is because of hard work and that luck has nothing to do with success. Although I believe that hard work is very important and is the **surest** way to success for most people, I must disagree with this **statement**. It cannot be denied that luck often plays an important role in success. For example, many important **discoveries** have been made by **accident**. There have been many **cases** of **researchers** and **inventors** making **major** breakthroughs while they were actually trying to solve another problem or **create** a different **device**.

Furthermore, there is something to be said for simply being in the right place at the right time — perhaps meeting someone by **chance** who can **offer** a good job or rare opportunity. And of course, there are the **rare** examples of **gamblers** and **lottery winners** who beat the **odds** and achieve **sudden** and **unexpected** success.

While the **influence** of luck cannot be **ignored**, this is not to say that one should **depend** on it and ignore the value of hard work. If one is **willing** to work hard, I believe that success will eventually be **achieved**, with or without the **added benefit** of luck. **Moreover**, hard work is often an essential **ingredient** of luck because it **enables** one to take **advantage** of a lucky encounter. If the scientist has not worked hard to develop his knowledge and **skills**, he may not **recognize** that lucky breakthrough when it comes along. **Therefore**, my suggestion is not to **count** on luck to **bring** you success. Instead, work hard and keep your eyes open for that lucky opportunity.

(296 words)

New Words

role	/rəʊl/	n.	作用;角色
luck	/lʌk/	n.	幸运, 运气
succeed	/sək'siːd/	v.	取得成功
disagree	/ˌdɪsə'griː/	v.	不同意,不赞同;与…不符合
★quotation	/kwəʊ'teɪʃn/	n.	引述, 引用语
sure	/ʃɔː/	a.	可靠的, 确实的
statement	/'steɪtmənt/	n.	陈述;声明
discovery	/dɪ'skʌvəri/	n.	发现;发觉
accident	/'æksɪdənt/	n.	意外,事故
case	/keɪs/	n.	事例, 案例;情况, 情形
researcher	/rɪ'sɜːtʃə/	n.	研究者
inventor	/ɪn'ventə/	n.	发明家,发明者
major	/'meɪdʒə/	a.	主要的, 较重要的
create	/kriː'eɪt/	v.	创造;产生, 引起
device	/dɪ'vaɪs/	n.	装置, 器具;方法
chance	/tʃɑːns/	n.	运气;机会
offer	/'ɒfə/	v.	提供
rare	/reə/	a.	极好的;稀罕的
▲gambler	/'gæmblə/	n.	赌徒
▲lottery	/'lɒtəri/	n.	彩票
winner	/'wɪnə/	n.	获胜者
▲odds	/ɒdz/	n.	可能性;机会

sudden	/ˈsʌdn/	a.	突然的
★unexpected	/ˌʌnɪkˈspektɪd/	a.	意料之外的，意想不到的
influence	/ˈɪnfluəns/	n.	作用；影响（力）
ignore	/ɪgˈnɔː/	v.	忽视，不理睬
depend	/dɪˈpend/	v.	取决于；依靠，依赖
willing	/ˈwɪlɪŋ/	a.	愿意的，乐意的；乐于助人的
achieve	/əˈtʃiːv/	v.	实现；获得，取得
add	/æd/	v.	附加，增加
benefit	/ˈbenɪfɪt/	n.	优良的条件；利益
moreover	/mɔːˈrəʊvə/	ad.	而且，此外
▲ingredient	/ɪnˈgriːdiənt/	n.	因素；组成部分
enable	/ɪˈneɪbl/	v.	使…能做某事；使…成为可能
advantage	/ədˈvɑːntɪdʒ/	n.	优势，益处
skill	/skɪl/	n.	技能，技艺
recognize	/ˈrekəgnaɪz/	v.	认出，识别出
★therefore	/ˈðeəfɔː/	ad.	因此
count	/kaʊnt/	v.	依靠，指望；数
bring	/brɪŋ/	v.	带来；引起

Phrases and Expressions

have nothing to do with	和…无关
play an important role in sth. /doing sth.	在…发挥重要作用
by accident / by chance	偶然地，意外地；碰巧
depend on / count on	依靠，依赖；指望
be willing to	愿意，乐意
take advantage of	利用；趁…之机
come along	出现，发生；进步，进展
keep one's eyes open for	留意，留心；密切注意

课文词数	生词总量	生词比率	二级词汇	三级词汇	超纲词汇
296	40	15.2%	33	3	4

Judge , according to the text , whether the following statements are True or False.

1. _____ Luck often plays an important role in success, so one can depend on it.

2. _____ As long as one is willing to work hard, success may be achieved in the end.

3. _____ There are many winners who beat the odds and succeed unexpectedly.

4. _____ Luck has such great influence on success that one should ignore the value of hard work.

5. _____ Hard work is essential to success because it enables one to take advantage of the lucky opportunity.

Unit 5 Friendship

TEXT A   The Elements of Friendship

When was the last time you made a friend? A friend is someone who is **honest** and you can **trust**. A friend is someone who you **hang** out with a lot, and someone you **rely** on. Friendship is being there for someone when they need you, and to have a common **bond** to have the **freedom** of hanging out with each other and to be comfortable around each other. The **main** ideas of friendship are **honesty** and trust, **caring** and having **similarities**.

Without honesty and trust, friendship wouldn't last very long. The **definition** of honesty is "**quality** and **condition** of being honest, **integrity**". Friendship would be held up by honesty. Trust is another important thing that **relates** to honesty, your friends really need to trust you. Honesty and trust are very important but so is caring.

You need to care for your friends so the **relationship** will last. The definition of caring is to be **concerned** for or interested in others. An example of care is being there when someone really needs you like during a bad situation. You should also be **supportive** of your friends. The definition of support is to take sides with or to provide help. **Even** though caring is important so are similarities in interest.

Similarities in friendship will make the bond grow. The definition of similarities is the quality or condition of being **alike**, **resemblance**. An example of similarities is two friends liking the same kind of music. Similarities in interests are things like a **couple** of friends liking the same thing like music, **hobbies** and many other things. It would help by making them want to do more things together.

Good friends will always use honesty and trust, caring and support, and similarities in interest if they want their friendship to last. Good friends never want to say goodbye!

(310 words)

New Words

element	/ˈelɪmənt/	n.	成分；要素
friendship	/ˈfrendʃɪp/	n.	友情，友爱
honest	/ˈɒnɪst/	a.	真诚的；正直的
trust	/trʌst/	n.	信用，信赖
		v.	信任，相信
hang	/hæŋ/	v.	挂；悬
rely	/rɪˈlaɪ/	v.	倚赖；信赖
★bond	/bɒnd/	n.	纽带；羁绊；束缚
		v.	接合
freedom	/ˈfrɪdəm/	n.	自由
main	/ˈmeɪn/	a.	主要的
honesty	/ˈɔnɪstɪ/	n.	诚实；正直
care	/keə/	v.	关心；照顾；喜爱；介意
		n.	小心；照料；忧虑
▲similarity	/ˌsɪmɪˈlærɪtɪ/	n.	相似（之处），类似（之处）
without	/wɪðˈaʊt/	prep.	没有
definition	/ˌdefɪˈnɪʃən/	n.	定义；清晰度
quality	/ˈkwɒlɪtɪ/	n.	特质；才能；品质
condition	/kənˈdɪʃən/	n.	情况；条件
▲integrity	/ɪnˈtegrɪtɪ/	n.	诚实；正直；完整；完善
relate	/rɪˈleɪt/	v.	使联系；有关系；讲，叙述
▲relationship	/rɪˈleɪʃənʃɪp/	n.	关系；关联
concern	/kənˈsɜːn/	n.	关心；关系；关切的事；忧虑
		v.	涉及；与…有关；影响；使关心
▲supportive	/səˈpɔːtɪv/	a.	支持的
even	/ˈiːvn/	ad.	甚至；恰好；正当
alike	/əˈlaɪk/	a.	相似的；同样的
resemblance	/rɪˈzembləns/	n.	相像
couple	/ˈkʌpl/	n.	对；夫妇；数个
hobby	/ˈhɒbɪ/	n.	业余爱好

Phrases and Expressions

rely on	依赖;信赖
hang out	闲逛;居住;挂出
hold up	举起;提出;抓举;支持住;阻挡
relate to	与…有关系
care for	关心;喜欢;介意
a couple of	两个;几个
take sides with	袒护;拥护
even though	即使

课文词数	生词总量	生词比率	二级词汇	三级词汇	超纲词汇
310	26	8.2%	21	1	4

GETTING THE MESSAGE

I. Recite the first paragraph of the text.

II. Decide which of the following best states the main idea of the passage.

A. The ways of making friends are different from people to people.

B. Friends should be honest to and trust each other.

C. The main ideas of friendship are honesty and trust, caring and having similarities.

D. What are honesty and trust, caring and support, and similarities in friendship?

III. Answer the following questions according to the text.

1. Do you have many friends around you?

2. What kind of person can you call a friend?

3. What do you do to your friend?

4. How do you make friends at university?

VOCABULARY AND STRUCTURE

I. Match words or phrases in Column A with their explanations in Column B.

A	B
1. bond	a. the feeling or relationship that exists between friends
2. relate to	b. straightforward; not cheating or stealing; not telling lies
3. friendship	c. to depend upon with confidence, look to for help
4. honest	d. to have reference to
5. rely on	e. a connection based on kinship, marriage or common interest
6. friend	f. an essential and distinguishing attribute of something or someone
7. concern	g. to support and sustain
8. hold up	h. to have to do with or be relevant to; be on the mind of
9. quality	i. to have a liking, fondness, or taste (for)
10. care for	j. a person you know well and regard with affection and trust

II. Fill in the blank in each sentence with a word or phrase taken from the box below. Change the word form if necessary.

hold up	bond	friendship	care for
honest	concern	relate to	quality

1. He shows _____ of leadership.
2. To be quite _____ with you, I don't think you can pass the examination.
3. Real _____ is more valuable than money.
4. These problems _____ all of us.
5. I decided to _____ on the news until he was sure of it.
6. A _____ of sympathy developed between members of the group.

III. Rewrite the following sentences after the model.

Model

Honesty and trust are very important *but* caring *is* very important *too*.
Honesty and trust are very important *but so is* caring.

1. Tom can speak English and French and Jack can speak both *too*.

_____

2. If you go to Jim's birthday party, I will *too*.

_____

If there was *no* honesty and trust, friendship wouldn't last very long.
Without honesty and trust, friendship wouldn't last very long.

3. If there was *no* sun, nothing would grow.

_____

4. He left the group of people but *did not* say anything.

_____

IV. Translate the following sentences into Chinese.

1. Friendship is being there for someone when they need you, and to have a common bond to have the freedom of hanging out with each other and to be comfortable around each other.

2. Friendship would be held up by honesty.

3. The definition of support is to take sides with or to provide help.

V. Translate the following sentences with words or phrases learnt in Text A.

1. 他的帮助是永远可依赖的。(rely on)

2. 我们应该改进所谓的生活品质。（quality）

3. 这两个事件相互有联系。（relate to）

4. 我患病期间她帮了我很大忙。（supportive）

5. 在那次争辩中，我支持他。（take sides with）

 **Speaking**

I. How to Ask for Help

When you ask for help, you should be polite and make sure the person you ask is able to give a hand. After that, you should express your gratitude.

Useful Sentence Patterns	
Sorry to interrupt you.	No trouble（bother）at all.
Sorry for bothering you.	Yes, sure.
I don't like to bother（trouble）you, but…	
Do you have time?	
Do you have a minute?	
Would you do me a favor?	I'd be glad to. What can I do?
Would you please lend me a hand?	Sorry, could you wait a minute? I'm tied up now.
Could I trouble you to…	Sure.
Would you mind if I use your…?	Go ahead.
	Of course not.
	I would like to but I'm very busy now.
	I'm very sorry. It's beyond me.

Model

Jane: Terry, would you do me a favor?

Terry: Sorry, a minute please. I'm answering a call. (A moment later) What do you want me to do?

Jane: See, I'm trying to make a cake. I need two cups of flour and two eggs. Will you bring me two eggs from the refrigerator?

Terry: Sure, anything else I can do for you?

Jane: Yes, put the egg in one bowl, and the flour in another.

Terry: Why are you making a cake?

Jane: Terry, today is Linda's birthday. I want to give her a happy surprise.

Terry: Ok, I'll keep it a secret.

II. How to Offer Help

Useful Sentence Patterns	
Can I help you? What can I do for you?	Yes, thank you very much. Just what I need.
Can I help you with… ? Is there anything I can do for you?	Yes, would you mind… for me?
Shall I do… for you? Would you like me to…?	Yes, of course. It's very kind of you. Thank you just the same. Thank you all the same.

Model

Johnny: Would you like me to help you with those packages?

Mark: Oh, yes. Thank you very much. It's very kind of you.

Johnny: No trouble at all. Are you parked nearby?

Mark: Right over there. The white truck.

Johnny: Can I help you put the packages into your truck?

Mark: Just what I need. In the front will be fine. Just let me open the door of it.

Johnny: Ok. Done.

Mark: Thanks again. You save me a lot of trouble.

III. Practice

1. Complete the following conversations and then act them out in pairs.

Example:

A: Hi, Miss White. Can you do me a favor?

B: Yes, of course.

1) Let me give you a hand.

   _____.

2) Would you like me to take you to that place?

   _____.

3) Would you kindly open the door for me?

   _____.

4) I'm wondering if you could do me a favor.

   _____.

5) Do you think you could possibly help me?

   _____.

6) Could I trouble you to shut the door?

   _____.

2. Complete the following conversations and then act them out in pairs.

1) Robert met Lisa at school.

   Robert: _____ with your foot?

Lisa: I fell down the steps just now.

Robert: _____ a look first. You might have broken a bone.

Lisa: Oh, it hurts very much. Could I _____ to take me to the hospital?

Robert: _____, no problem.

Lisa: _____. It's very kind of you.

2) Black visited Juliet who was under treatment at hospital.

Black: Good morning. Are you hungry? _____ to make you something to eat?

Juliet: No, _____, Black. I'm not very hungry, but thank you _____.

Black: Isn't there _____ for you?

Juliet: Well, yes. _____ buying some fruits for me? Some apples, I think.

Black: No, _____. Anything else?

Juliet: _____, thanks a lot. Oh, there's just one more thing. _____ you could go to the post office for me.

Black: I'm sorry. _____ I can't tonight. I have to meet Mort in ten minutes. But I could go tomorrow after work.

Juliet: Oh, that's OK. _____.

Black: I'll drop in and see you tomorrow then, Juliet. See you, bye.

3. Work in pairs. Practise offering help to your partner according to the situations below. Then switch roles.

1) You are working at the office and are very busy, so you need some help from your workmate, Bill, who is free now.

2) Sally is a freshman in a university. She has a bad stomachache. Lucy is her roommate who is trying to offer some help.

B Listening

Listen to the 10 conversations and choose the best answer to each question.

1. A. Wife and husband.   B. Shop assistant and customer.   C. Waitress and customer.

2. A. At a booking office.   B. In a library.   C. At a bank.

3. A. At a gas station.   B. At a bank.   C. At a hospital.

4. A. Physics test.   B. Physical heath.   C. English test.

5. A. 7 o'clock.   B. 6:45.   C. 6:55.

6. A. An operator.   B. A salesgirl.   C. A waitress.

7. A. In a grocery store.   B. In a restaurant.   C. In a department store.

8. A. Ask the air hostess for a change.

   B. Move to another part of the plane.

   C. Put out his cigarette.

9. A. She can borrow the dictionary.

   B. She cannot borrow the dictionary now.

   C. The dictionary has been borrowed by his roommate.

10. A. The woman will post the letter for him.

    B. The woman will go to the man's office.

    C. The woman will not post the letter for him.

Sounds and Spellings

I. Listen and practice. Pay special attention to the pronunciation of the italicized letters.

1. / l /   fee*l*, we*ll*
2. /r/   *r*ead, so*rr*y
3. /e/   y*e*t, f*e*w, c*u*re
4. /w/   *wh*en, a*w*ay, pers*u*ade

II. Listen and practice. Pay special attention to the pronunciation of the plosives in continuous speech.

1. Wine and judgment mature with age.   酒老味醇,人老识深。
2. Charity begins at home.   仁爱先施与亲友。
3. Don't cry over spilt milk.   别作无意义的后悔。
4. A near friend is better than a far-dwelling kinsman.   远亲不如近友。
5. One of the greatest pleasures in life is conversation.   生活中最大的乐趣之一是交谈。

III. Read and enjoy.

> A little boy asked his father: Daddy, how much does it cost to get married?
> The father replied: I don't know son. I'm still paying!
>
> ☺☺☺☺☺

 Grammar

I. Fill in the blanks with a word given.

1. Fruit is rich _____ vitamins. (in, of)
2. She was quick _____ bringing the dinner. (about, at)
3. His secret was safe _____ them. (from, with)
4. Is the city famous _____ the prosperity of its agriculture? (for, to)
5. I'm useless _____ anything electrical. (at, on)
6. I believe they are related _____ the project. (for, to)
7. The poor girl always relies _____ her step-mother after her father's death. (upon, to)
8. Friends should care _____ each other. (of, for)
9. Who were you talking _____ just now on the phone? (to, at)
10. He came to the meeting _____ his serious illness. (except, despite)

II. Choose the one that best completes the sentence among the four choices marked A , B , C and D below each sentence.

1. The students were in favor _____ reform.
   A. to   B. off   C. on   D. of
2. Don't count _____ him. He is not reliable.
   A. for   B. on   C. with   D. in
3. Mary changed her green skirt _____ a red one today.
   A. for   B. in   C. into   D. at
4. I think it wrong _____ him not to accept our invitation.
   A. to   B. for   C. of   D. with
5. Every speech at the meeting is limited _____ 20 minutes.
   A. in   B. on   C. at   D. to

6. The manager should act _____ the suggestions the experts made.

    A. on   B. for   C. out of   D. from

7. I should remind you that it is _____ my power to change your fate, though I would very much like to.

    A. within   B. out of   C. off   D. beyond

8. Peter is always open _____ suggestions from his fellow workers.

    A. for   B. on   C. to   D. into

9. They are pretty sharp and she'll have to be _____ her best to keep up with them.

    A. at   B. in   C. for   D. on

10. I have just been in to see if I can be _____ any assistance to them.

    A. at   B. of   C. with   D. in

Writing

I. General Writing

1. Read the following private letter from Zhang Li to her old friend and then write a short letter to one of your classmates.

Sample

No. 4, Jianguo Rd, Shanghai

May 24th, 2003

Dear Judy,

    It has been half a year since you left for America. I miss you very much. Luckily, I'll come to New York to attend a meeting on May 10th. The meeting will last for five days. I will come to see you during my stay in New York and we can have a good talk.

    I'm looking forward to seeing you!

                                Yours,

                                Zhang Li

2. Read the following sample and then write a thank-you letter to one of your friends. It can be a thank-you letter for a meal, being entertained, a visit or any other occasion, using expressions such as:

Thank you for...

Thank you very much for...

I am most/extremely grateful for...

It was very good/nice of you to...

This is to tender our deep gratitude for...

 ## Sample

London, Britain

Dear Alex,

This is just a short letter to thank you again for all the work you put into organizing my time in Beijing. I especially enjoyed having dinner with you and your family. Thanks also for getting me tickets to the theater to watch Beijing opera.

I really enjoyed my time in Beijing. It was great to see all my old friends again and I also appreciated Beijing opera very much. I hope I'll be back soon!

Next time you're in London, I'd be pleased to show you around and take you out to dinner.

Best wishes,

Jenny Smith

II. Writing for Specific Purposes

Have you ever written on an envelope in English? If not, here are some tips for you:

1. Put the name and address of the letter writer in the top left corner or on the back of the envelope.

2. Put the name and address of the addressee in the middle of the envelope.

3. Stick a stamp in the top right corner of the envelope.

4. When you write the address of addressee or letter writer, follow the order of: name, house or building number, street or road, city, province or state, zip code, country.

5. Use the title before name of the addressee such as Mr., Mrs., Miss., Ms., Dr. or Prof.

Read the following sample to learn how to address an envelope. Then write an envelope yourself.

Sample

Ms. Wang Xiaolan
15 Huaihai Street   *Stamp*
Shanghai 210088
China

> Peter Brown
> 22 Blackpool Road
> Sydney 2140
> Australia

TEXT B   How to Mend a Broken Friendship

By Patricia Skalka

There's no better time than the present to make **amends** with old **pals**. Here's how to get past the **grudge** and **reclaim** the relationships that bring joy and **laughter** to your life.

Reach out to old friends. Growing up across the street from each other in Twin Falls, Idaho, Lisa Fry and Paula Turner never **doubted** their friendship would last forever. But after Fry married, moved to New York City and had a baby, her letters to Turner suddenly went unanswered. "Do you think I've **somehow offended** her?" Fry asked her husband.

Turner, **meanwhile**, had **convinced** herself she was no longer important to Fry. "She's got a family now," she told herself. "We're just too different to be close like before."

Finally, Fry **summoned** the **courage** to call her old friend. At first, the conversation was **awkward**, yet soon they both admitted that they missed each other. A month later, they got together and quickly fell into their old habit of laughing and **sharing** confidences.

"Thank **goodness** I finally took action," Fry says, "We both **realized** we were as important to each other as ever."

There are good reasons to **cherish** our friendships. Some years ago a public-opinion **research firm**, Roper Starch Worldwide, asked 2007 people to **identify** one or two things that said the most about themselves. Friends far **outranked** homes, jobs, clothes and cars.

"A well-established friendship carries a long history of experience and **interaction** that **defines** who we are and keeps us connected," says Donald Pannen, **executive** officer of the Western Psychological Association. "It is a **heritage** we should **protect**."

Ironically, says Brant R. Burleson, professor of **communication** at Purdue University in West Lafayette, Ind., "the better friends you are, the more likely you'll face **conflicts**." And the **outcome** can be precisely what you don't want — an end to the relationship.

(305 words)

New Words

mend	/mend/	v.	修补,修理
★amend	/əˈmend/	v.	改良;改善;修正;改正
▲pal	/pæl/	n.	朋友;同志
▲grudge	/grʌdʒ/	n.	怨恨;恶意;嫉妒;遗恨
		v.	不愿给;吝惜
▲reclaim	/rɪˈkleɪm/	v.	改正;矫正;开拓
laughter	/ˈlɑːftə/	n.	笑
doubt	/daʊt/	v.	怀疑;不相信;不能确定
somehow	/ˈsʌmhaʊ/	adv.	说不上什么理由;反正
offend	/əˈfend/	v.	伤…的感情;触怒;犯法,犯罪
meanwhile	/ˈmiːnwaɪl/	adv.	其时,此际
convince	/kənˈvɪns/	v.	使(某人)信服;使(某人)明白
▲summon	/ˈsʌmən/	v.	召唤;传唤;召集;聚集
courage	/ˈkʌreɪdʒ/	n.	勇气,勇敢
★awkward	/ˈɔːkwəd/	a.	尴尬的;不方便的;笨拙的
share	/ʃeə/	v.	分享;分给;分配;共有;共用
		n.	一份;与他人分摊的股份或利润;股票
▲goodness	/ˈɡʊdnɪs/	n.	用以代替 God;善良;美德
realize	/ˈrɪəlaɪz/	v.	认识到;了解到;实现
▲cherish	/ˈtʃerɪʃ/	v.	珍惜;爱惜

research	/rɪˈsɜːtʃ/	n.	调查;研究;探索
		v.	从事研究工作
firm	/fɜːm/	n.	公司;厂商
		a.	坚固的,坚实的;坚定的;稳定的
★identify	/aɪˈdentɪfaɪ/	v.	认出;鉴定;与…认同
▲outrank	/aʊtˈræŋk/	v.	阶级高于;地位高于
interaction	/ɪntərˈækʃn/	n.	相互影响;相互作用
★define	/dɪˈfaɪn/	v.	界定,定义;限定,规定
★executive	/ɪɡˈzekjʊtɪv/	a.	执行的;实行的
▲heritage	/ˈherɪtɪdʒ/	n.	遗产,继承物
protect	/prəˈtekt/	v.	保护;防御
▲ironically	/aɪˈrɒnɪklɪ/	adv.	讽刺地,用反语地
communication	/kəˌmjuːnɪˈkeɪʃn/	n.	公共关系;传播;信息;通讯;交通
★conflict	/ˈkɒnflɪkt/	n.	争执;冲突;抵触;战斗;斗争
		v.	(与…)相反;抵触;冲突
★outcome	/ˈaʊtkʌm/	n.	结果;成果;结局

课文词数	生词总量	生词比率	二级词汇	三级词汇	超纲词汇
305	31	10.2%	15	7	9

Judge, according to the text, whether the following statements are True or False.

1. _____ Fry and Turner once doubted if they would not be friends any longer after Fry had a baby.
2. _____ Turner didn't answer Fry's letters because Fry once offended her.
3. _____ Fry summoned the courage to call her old friends to convince Turner.
4. _____ After the call, Fry and Turner are good friends again and cherish their friendship as ever.
5. _____ The research reports that most people think family and job are more important than friends.

Unit 6 Sports

TEXT A Revival of the Olympic Games

In the seventeenth **century**, the Olympic **Games** sports **festival** was held in England, followed by the **National** Olympic Games, which were **established** in the nineteenth century and continue to this day. Later, **similar** events were **organized** in France and Greece, but these were all small-**scale** and **certainly** not **international**.

The interest in **reviving** the Olympics as an international event grew when the **ruins** of **ancient** Olympia were **uncovered** by German **archaeologists** in the **mid** nineteenth century. At the same time, Baron Pierre de Coubertin was **searching** for a **reason** for the French **defeat** in the Franco-Prussian War (1870—1871). He thought the reason was that the French had not **received proper** physical education, and **sought** to improve this. In 1890 he attended the Wenlock Olympian **Society**. Coubertin also thought of a way to bring **nations** closer together, to have the youth of the **world compete** in sports, rather than fight in war. In his eyes, the **recovery** of the Olympic Games would achieve both of these **goals**.

In a **congress** at the Sorbonne University, in Paris, held from June 16 to June 23, 1894, he **presented** his ideas to an international **audience**. On the last day of the congress, it was decided that the first **modern** Olympic Games would take place in 1896 in Athens, in the country of their birth. To organize the Games, the International Olympic **Committee** (IOC) was established, with the Greek Demetrius Vikelas as its first **president**.

The **total** number of **athletes** at the the first modern Olympic Games, less than 250, seems small by modern **standards**, but the games were the largest international sports event ever held until that time. The Greek **officials** and **public** were also very **enthusiastic**, and they even **proposed** to have the **monopoly** of organizing the Olympics. The IOC decided **differently**, however, and the second Olympic Games took place in Paris, France. Paris was also the first Olympic Games where women were **allowed** to compete.

(324 words)

New Words

▲revival	/rɪˈvaɪvl/	n.	复苏;振兴
century	/ˈsentʃəri/	n.	世纪;百年
game	/geɪm/	n.	体育运动;游戏
festival	/ˈfestɪvl/	n.	(音乐、戏剧、电影等的)节;节日
national	/ˈnæʃnəl/	a.	国家的;全国的
establish	/ɪˈstæblɪʃ/	v.	建立;创立
similar	/ˈsɪmələ/	a.	类似的;相像的
organize	/ˈɔːgənaɪz/	v.	组织;筹备
scale	/skeɪl/	n.	规模;程度
certainly	/ˈsɜːtnli/	ad.	肯定;当然
international	/ɪntəˈnæʃnəl/	a.	国际的
▲revive	/rɪˈvaɪv/	v.	(使)复兴;使重做
ruin	/ˈruːɪn/	n.	残垣断壁;废墟
ancient	/ˈeɪnʃənt/	a.	古代的;古老的
uncover	/ʌnˈkʌvə/	v.	发现
▲archaeologist	/ɑːkɪˈɒlədʒɪst/	n.	考古学家
mid	/mɪd/	n.	居中;在中间　a. 居中的;在中间的
search	/sɜːtʃ/	v.	查找;搜索　n. 查找;搜索
reason	/ˈriːzn/	n.	原因;理由
defeat	/dɪˈfiːt/	n.	战败;失败　v. 击败;战胜
receive	/rɪˈsiːv/	v.	接到;收到
proper	/ˈprɒpə/	a.	恰当的
seek	/siːk/ (sought/sɔːt/, sought) v.	寻求;试图;设法
society	/səˈsaɪəti/	n.	协会;社会

nation	/ˈneɪʃn/	n.	国家
world	/wɜːld/	n.	世界
compete	/kəmˈpiːt/	v.	竞争
recovery	/rɪˈkʌvəri/	n.	恢复
goal	/gəʊl/	n.	目标
congress	/ˈkɒŋgres/	n.	代表大会
present	/prɪˈzent/	v.	提出;提交
	/ˈprezent/	a.	现存的;当前的　　n. 礼物;礼品
audience	/ˈɔːdiəns/	n.	观众;听众
modern	/ˈmɒdn/	a.	近代的;现代的
committee	/kəˈmɪti/	n.	委员会
president	/ˈprezɪdənt/	n.	主席;总统
total	/ˈtəʊtl/	a.	总的;总计的
athlete	/ˈæθliːt/	n.	运动员
standard	/ˈstændəd/	n.	标准
official	/əˈfɪʃl/	n.	官员　　a. 官方的;正式的
public	/ˈpʌblɪk/	n.	民众　　a. 大众的;公众的
enthusiastic	/ɪnˌθjuːzɪˈæstɪk/	a.	热情的;热心的
propose	/prəˈpəʊz/	v.	提议;建议
▲monopoly	/məˈnɒpəli/	n.	垄断;专营服务
differently	/ˈdɪfrəntli/	ad.	不同地
allow	/əˈlaʊ/	v.	允许;准许

Phrases and Expressions

at the same time	同时;不过
search for sth/sb	查找;搜查
think of	想出;想起某事
rather than	而不是;宁愿…(而不愿…)
in one's eyes/in the eyes of	在某人看来
take place	发生;进行
less than	小于;少于

Proper Names

France	法国

Greece	希腊
Olympia	奥林匹亚(古地名,位于希腊伯罗奔尼撒半岛西部,皮尔戈斯城东。古希腊著名宗教圣地,有古希腊神宇斯庙和希拉庙等古迹。奥林匹克运动的发祥地。)
Baron Pierre de Coubertin	拜伦·皮埃尔·德·顾拜旦(1863—1937,法国贵族,现代奥运会的创始人)
Franco-Prussian War	普法战争(1870—1871 年法国和普鲁士之间的战争,以法军战败,签订《法兰克福和约》结束。战后,普鲁士统一了德意志。)
Demetrius Vikelas	德米特留斯·维凯拉斯(1835—1908),希腊诗人和教育家,国际奥委会首任主席(1894—1896)
Paris	巴黎(法国首都)

课文词数	生词总量	生词比率	二级词汇	三级词汇	超纲词汇
324	45	13.9%	41		4

GETTING THE MESSAGE

I. Recite the third paragraph of the text.

II. Decide which of the following best states the main idea of the passage.

    A. Why the first modern Olympic Games took place in 1896.

    B. What did people do in the first modern Olympic Games.

    C. The article describes the process of the revival of the modern Olympic Games.

    D. Why Demetrius Vikelas was chosen as the first president of the first modern Olympic Games.

III. Answer the following questions.

1. Were sports events organized on a large scale in France and Greece?

2. Did the French receive proper education?

3. For what purpose was the International Olympic Committee (IOC) established?

4. What kind of sports do you like best and why?

=== **VOCABULARY AND STRUCTURE** ===

I. Match words or phrases in Column A with their explanations in Column B.

A	B
1. differently	a. a period of 100 years
2. search	b. to start or create an organization, a system, etc. that is meant to last for a long time
3. century	c. like sb./sth. but not exactly the same
4. total	d. to look carefully for sth./sb.
5. modern	e. the size or extent of sth., especially when compared with sth. else
6. establish	f. being the amount or number after everyone or everything is counted or added together
7. mid	g. not the same as sb./sth.; not like sb./sth. else
8. scale	h. of the present time or recent times
9. similar	i. the Earth, with all its countries, peoples and the natural features
10. world	j. in the middle of

II. Fill in the blank in each sentence with a word or phrase taken from the box below. Change the word form if necessary.

> organize, think of, rather than, standard, audience, propose, take place, allow

1. The _____ enjoyed the concert very much last night.
2. A serious car accident _____ on the highway this morning because of the thick fog.
3. The sports meet _____ very well.
4. I will go to meet him _____ wait for him.
5. I never _____ doing such a thing.
6. Children are not _____ to swim in this river.

III. Rewrite the following sentences after the model.

 **Model**

He didn't pass the English exam *because* he didn't study hard.
The reason for his failure in the English exam was that he didn't study hard.

1. The little girl was happy *because* her mother bought a new dress for her.

   _____.

2. I choose computer science as my major *because* I like it very much.

   _____.

Tom said he would go out to play after he had done his homework.
Tom said he. would not go out to play until he had done his homework.

3. My mother started to watch TV after she had washed dishes.

   _____.

4. He came only after the class was over.

   _____.

IV. Translate the following sentences into Chinese.

1. Later, similar events were organized in France and Greece, but these were all small-scale and certainly not international.

2. The interest in reviving the Olympics as an international event grew when the ruins of ancient Olympia were uncovered by German archaeologists in the mid nineteenth century.

3. The IOC decided differently, however, and the second Olympic Games took place in Paris, France.

V. Translate the following sentences with words or phrases we have learnt in the text.

1. 我宁愿煮饭也不愿意打扫房间。(rather than)

2. 这所学校的学生人数不到300人。（less than）

3. 在她父亲的帮助下，她建立了自己的公司。（establish）

4. 他建议我们去看老师，因老师生病了。（propose）

5. 近年来成都发生了巨大变化。（take place）

 **Speaking**

I. How to Ask Directions

When asking directions, you should pay attention to the following:

☺ It is necessary to be polite when asking directions. It is better to stop walking and wait for a person you would like to ask or walk to him/her but in no rush, otherwise the person would doubt your motive.

☺ Don't stretch out your hand and put it on the person's shoulder or arm, for this would be considered impolite.

☺ Keep a certain distance from the person, especially when it is a woman, so that he/she would not feel embarrassed or even threatened.

☺ You should say "Excuse me", or "Could you help me?" etc. to start the conversation. By saying so, you can attract the attention of the person politely.

☺ At the end of the conversation, you should say such words as "Many thanks", "Thanks a lot," etc.

Useful Sentence Patterns

Excuse me, please. Could you tell me how to get to the bus station? Excuse me, can you please tell me where the station is? Excuse me, but I'm trying to find the bus station.	Turn round and turn left at the traffic lights. Take the second on the left and then ask again. Go down the street and take the third turn on the right. First right, second left. You can't miss it.
Will it take me long to get there? Is it far? Should I take a bus? Is it too far to walk?	No, it's only two hundred meters. No, it's only about five minutes' walk. No, you can walk it in under three minutes. No, it's no distance at all.
Many thanks. Thank you. Thank you very much indeed. Thanks a lot.	It's a pleasure. That's quite all right. That's OK. Not at all.

Model 1

Zhang Hua: Excuse me. Is there a McDonald's around here?

Jiang Dong: Yes, but it's a bit far from here.

Zhang Hua: Well, my little daughter likes to eat there and we are strangers here. Would you please let us know how we can get there?

Jiang Dong: First you have to walk along the street for about 100 meters, then you take the No. 18 bus on your right.

Zhang Hua: How many stops will it be?

Jiang Dong: Oh, it's three stops.

Zhang Hua: Thanks very much.

Model 2

Peng Yun: Excuse me, Miss, where is the No. 7 bus stop?

Zhao Wen: Which direction are you going in?

Peng Yun: I'm going downtown.

Zhao Wen: Just stand over there across the street in front of the library.

Peng Yun: Thank you very much.

II. Practice

1. Complete the following conversations and then act them out in pairs.

1) The man wants to go to the nearest computer shop.

Yu Tao: Pardon me. Could you _____ tell me where the nearest computer shop _____?

Liao Yue: Sure. Go _____ the street.

Yu Tao: Do I _____ the second turning on the right?

Liao Yue: No, you want the first on the _____.

Yu Tao: Thanks a lot.

2) The woman wants to find Sichuan University.

An Ni: _____ me. Would you mind _____ me how to get to Sichuan University? I'm a _____ here.

Zheng Hao: Certainly. You should _____ the No. 12 bus opposite the road.

An Ni: How many _____ shall I have from here?

Zheng Hao: I'm not so _____, but you can ask the conductor.

An Ni: Thank you _____.

Zheng Hao: That's all right.

2. Work in pairs. Practise asking directions with your partner according to the situations below. Then switch roles.

1) Liu Gang is in the centre of the city, and he is asking the directions to the zoo.

2) Miss Yu comes out of Chengdu Railway Station, and she wants to get to the Tianfu Square.

B Listening

Listen to the four conversations and choose the best answer to each question.

1. A. The town.　　　　B. The countryside.　　　C. The town centre.
2. A. A couple of hundred yards.
   B. A few yards.
   C. A few miles
3. A. One turn.　　　　B. Three turns.　　　　C. Two turns.
4. A. She can get there by bus.
   B. She can get there on foot.
   C. She can get there by bike.
5. A. Second.　　　　B. Third.　　　　C. First.
6. A. Ten minutes.　　　B. About five minutes.　　　C. About three minutes.
7. A. The school.　　　B. The station.　　　C. The park.
8. A. No distance at all.　　B. It's a long distance.　　C. It's a little bit far.

C Sounds and Spellings

I. Listen and practise. Pay special attention to the pronunciation of the italicized letters.

1. /iː/	h*e*, *ea*t, s*ee*, f*ie*ld, rec*ei*ve, k*ey*
2. /ɪ/	*i*t, sh*i*p, c*i*ty, pr*e*tty, v*i*llage
3. /e/	b*e*d, h*ea*d, m*a*ny
4. /æ/	c*a*t
5. /ɜː/	w*o*rd, b*i*rd, *ea*rth, b*u*rn, j*ou*rney
6. /ə/	m*o*ther, doct*or*, *a*bove, cust*o*m, begg*ar*, poss*i*ble, s*u*ppose, fam*ou*s, lab*ou*r, nat*u*re, centr*e*
7. /ʌ/	c*u*t, l*o*ve, bl*oo*d, y*ou*ng

II. Listen and practice.

1. A mother's love never changes.　母爱永恒。

2. Blood is thicker than water.　血浓于水。

3. Custom makes all things easy.　有个好习惯,事事皆不难。

4. Learn young, learn fair.　学习趁年轻,学要学好。

5. Wisdom in the mind is better than money in the hand.　胸中有知识,胜于手中有金钱。

III. Read and enjoy.

"Do you believe in life after death?" the boss asked one of his employees.

"Yes, Sir." the new recruit replied.

"Well, then, that makes everything just fine," the boss went on. "After you left early yesterday to go to your grandmother's funeral, she stopped in to see you."

D Grammar

I. Fill in the blanks with the words given and change the word form when necessary.

1. They live in a big, _____ house. (red)

2. The camel is a very _____ animal. (use)

3. This plant has _____ flowers. (yellow, small)

4. Is that _____(brown) table _____? (big)

5. These apples have a _____ taste. (sweet)

6. _____ (he) mother told the little boy an _____ (interest) story.

7. It started to become _____ (cold) again yesterday.

8. Have you seen a _____ (white) cat? Our cat is missing.

9. The girl got _____ (fright) when the man began to walk toward her.

10. _____ (what) book are you reading now?

II. Choose the answer which best completes the following sentences.

1. _____ students are there in _____ class?
   - A. How much, your
   - B. What, you
   - C. How many, you
   - D. How many, your

2. The soup smells _____.
   - A. well
   - B. good
   - C. goodness
   - D. goodish

3. It is _____ for old people to walk on _____ roads.
   - A. dangerous, icy
   - B. danger, icy
   - C. dangerous, ice
   - D. danger, ice

4. _____ do you like best?
   - A. What sport
   - B. How sport
   - C. How many sports
   - D. For what sport

5. Is there _____ with the recorder?
   - A. some wrong
   - B. wrong something
   - C. anything wrong
   - D. wrong anything

6. These children look _____.
   - A. happy and health
   - B. happiness and healthy
   - C. happy and healthy
   - D. happiness and health

7. A _____ chair stood against the wall.
   - A. breaking
   - B. broken
   - C. broke
   - D. break

8. _____, among those boys, is your younger brother?
   - A. What one
   - B. How one
   - C. Why
   - D. Which one

9. Students should keep their rooms _____.
   - A. clean and tidy
   - B. clean and tide
   - C. cleaning and tidy
   - D. cleaning and tide

10. We have learned _____ skills from the workers there.
   - A. important many
   - B. many important
   - C. many importance
   - D. much important

Writing

I. Tips for writing E-mails

E-mails, compared with the traditional hand-written letters, are often regarded as conversations. Thus it is often not necessary to use formal language in e-mails. But for good e-mails, the following should be paid attention to:

1. Give the message a short and clear subject/title.

2. Start the message with a greeting so as to help create a friendly tone.

3. Start with a clear indication of what the message is about in the first paragraph.

4. End the message in a polite way. Common endings are: Yours sincerely, Best regards, Best wishes, Regards, etc.

5. Include your name at the end of the message.

II. Writing task

Read the following e-mail and then write an e-mail to your friend describing a sport you like. You are required to read it aloud in class next time.

Dear Tim:

    How are things going with you now? You know I like playing football very much. It's very good that our school holds football matches on campus in October every year. And this year I was trying hard to play well as a right winger (右边锋). But I don't think our team cooperated as well as we did in the last season. I feel sorry that finally our team only got fourth, and we usually get first.

Take care!

Yours,

Tom

TEXT B A Woman at the Wheel

The **pits** at the **race track** were very busy. **Drivers** and **engineers** were working hard on their **powerful** racing cars. The engine is the most important **part** of a racing car and the engineers in the pits were men who were caring for the engines. Each racing **team** had its own pit: there was **fuel** and oil for the cars, a **workshop**, **spare** parts… The drivers were all young men, **except** one. That was Lella Lombardi.

Miss Lombardi is a young Italian woman. She is small but **strong**; and she is a good racing driver. She is the only woman whom you might see at the wheel of a modern racing car.

"I've been in love with fast cars all my life," she says, "I always wanted to be a racing driver." She used to work for her father in his **meat** business. Sometimes she drove one of his meat **lorries**. This, of course, gave her the driving experience. At that time she **saved** as much money as possible. Then, in 1965, she bought her first racing car. It was a small car that cost about £ 500. She drove it in two races, and her parents did not know. She **won** her third race — and after that everyone knew her name!

Since then Lella Lombardi has owned several racing cars. Each car has been bigger and faster than the one before. At first men drivers did not like to race against a woman. But they have had to change their **minds**. Miss Lombardi now drives some of the fastest cars in the world.

Have a look at the newspapers in the **motor** racing season. You will be sure to see her name. It is possible that she will win one or two important races.

New Words

wheel	/wiːl/	n.	方向盘;车轮
▲ pit	/pɪt/	n.	(赛车道旁的)修理加油站
race	/reɪs/	n.	速度竞赛
★ track	/træk/	n.	(赛跑、赛车等的)跑道
driver	/ˈdraɪvə/	n.	驾驶员;司机
engineer	/ˌendʒɪˈnɪə/	n.	工程师;机修工
powerful	/ˈpauəfl/	a.	强有力的,强大的
part	/pɑːt/	n.	部件;零件

team	/tiːm/	*n.*	（游戏或运动的）队
fuel	/fjuːəl/	*n.*	燃料
★workshop	/ˈwɜːkʃɒp/	*n.*	车间；工场
spare	/speə/	*a.*	备用的
except	/ɪkˈsept/	*prep.*	（用于所言不包括的人或事物前）除…之外
strong	/strɒŋ/	*a.*	强壮的
meat	/miːt/	*n.*	肉（类）
lorry	/ˈlɒri/	*n.*	（英）运货汽车，卡车
save	/seɪv/	*v.*	攒钱
cost	/kɒst/	*v.*	需付费；价钱为 *n.* 费用，价钱
win	/wɪn/	*v.*	（在比赛、赛跑、战斗等中）获胜，赢
		n.	（比赛、竞赛等中的）胜利，赢
mind	/maɪnd/	*n.*	头脑；大脑
		v.	（尤用于疑问句或否定句，不用于被动句）对…介意
motor	/ˈməʊtə/	*n.*	汽车；发动机

Phrases and Expressions

race track	赛道
care for	照看
spare parts	备用部件
of course	（强调所说的话真实或正确）当然
change one's mind	改变决定（或看法、主意）
have a look at	看一看

课文词数	生词总量	生词比率	二级词汇	三级词汇	超纲词汇
304	21	6.9%	18	2	1

Judge , according to the text , whether the following statements are True or False.

1. _____ The engine is the most important part of a racing car.

2. _____ A racing team doesn't need its own pit.

3. _____ Among the participants in the car racing , most drivers were young men.

4. _____ The first racing car Miss Lombardi bought was a small one.

5. _____ Lella Lombardi has several racing cars and each car is bigger but slower than the one before.

Leisure Time

TEXT A   The Problem of Leisure

The **problem** of **leisure** is new. Until very **recent** times people worked each day to the **limit** of their strength. Of course there were always a privileged few who had leisure; but most men had to work 12, 14, or even 16 hours a day, six days a week. As late as 1840 the **average** factory worker **labored** 72 hours a week. "**Sunup** to **sundown**" was the farmer's day, or as another **phrase puts** it, "from can to can't."

Today, working less than a 40-hour week, people **enjoy** more leisure time. **Hence**, the **wise use** of leisure time has become an important problem for everyone, young or old. It is a **particularly** difficult problem for the sick, the **aged**, and those who have **retired** from earning a **living**. Those people have **so** much leisure that it is hard for them to find interesting and **worthwhile** ways to use it.

However short the work week becomes, work is still the most important part of life. We do not work to get leisure and the **pleasures** leisure brings us; rather, we use leisure **wisely** so that work itself can become **rewarding** and **enjoyable**. The **feeling** of success at doing one's **daily** work — **whether** it is a job, **maintaining** a home, or going to school — depends **largely** on coming to it each day with fresh **energy** and active interest.

Leisure and **recreation** go **together**, though they are not **necessarily** the same thing. "Recreation" has an obvious **meaning**. It is the kind of leisure **activity** that brings "re-creation" of **strength** and **spirit**. When one speaks of making good use of leisure, he means choosing **recreational** activities, which contribute to health, growth, and spirit.

(283 words)

New Words

problem	/ˈprɒbləm/	n.	问题;难题
leisure	/ˈleʒə/	n.	空闲;闲暇
recent	/ˈriːsnt/	a.	新近的;近来的
limit	/ˈlɪmɪt/	n.	界限,限度;(pl.)范围 v. 限制,限定
strength	/streŋθ/	a.	力,力量,力气
★privilege	/ˈprɪvəlɪdʒ/	vt.	给与…特权,特免 n. 特权,优惠
average	/ˈævərɪdʒ/	a.	一般的,通常的,平均的 n. 平均
factory	/ˈfæktri/	n.	工厂;制造厂
labor	/ˈleɪbə/	v.	劳动,努力争取(for) n. 劳动;努力
week	/wiːk/	n.	星期,周
▲sunup	/ˈsʌnʌp/	n.	日出
▲sundown	/ˈsʌndaʊn/	n.	日落
phrase	/freɪz/	n.	短语;习语;惯用语
put	/pʊt/	v.	表达;放,摆,安置
enjoy	/ɪnˈdʒɔɪ/	v.	享受…的乐趣;欣赏,喜爱
★hence	/hens/	ad.	因此,从此
wise	/waɪz/	a.	英明的,明智的
use	/juːz/	n.	使用;利用;用途 v. 使用;利用
particularly	/pəˈtɪkjələli/	ad.	特别,尤其
aged	/eɪdʒd/	a.	年老的;老年人特有的
retire	/rɪˈtaɪə/	v.	退休,引退
living	/ˈlɪvɪŋ/	n.	生活,生计 a. 活的;现存的
so	/səʊ/	ad.	[表示程度]如此,那么;
			[表示方式]这样,那样,如此,因此
★worthwhile	/ˌwɜːθˈwaɪl/	a.	值得做的,值得出力的
pleasure	/ˈpleʒə/	n.	愉快,快乐;乐事,乐趣
wisely	/ˈwaɪzli/	ad.	明智地,聪明地
rewarding	/rɪˈwɔːdɪŋ/	a.	有益的;有价值的
enjoyable	/ɪnˈdʒɔɪəbl/	a.	令人愉快的;可享受的
feeling	/ˈfiːlɪŋ/	n.	感觉;情绪;同情
daily	/ˈdeɪli/	a.	日常的,每日的
whether	/ˈweðə/	conj.	是否;不管,无论
maintain	/meɪnˈteɪn/	v.	维持;维修

largely	/ˈlɑːdʒli/	ad.	很大程度上，主要地
energy	/ˈenədʒi/	n.	精力，精神；活力
▲ recreation	/ˌrekriˈeɪʃn/	n.	消遣，娱乐
together	/təˈgeðə/	ad.	在一起
necessarily	/ˌnesəˈserəli/	ad.	必要地
meaning	/ˈmiːnɪŋ/	n.	意义；含意
activity	/ækˈtɪvəti/	n.	活动；活动性
strength	/strenθ/	n.	力量，力气；实力
spirit	/ˈspɪrɪt/	n.	精神；灵魂
▲ recreational	/ˌrekriˈeɪʃənl/	a.	休养的；娱乐的

Phrases and Expressions

to the limit of	到极点
earn one's living	谋生
so that	以便
daily work	日常工作
go together	［口］经常做伴；形影不离；陪同；相配
speak of	谈及，说到
make use of	利用；使用
contribute to	起作用，有助于；作出贡献

课文词数	生词总量	生词比率	二级词汇	三级词汇	超纲词汇
283	45	15.9%	38	3	4

GETTING THE MESSAGE

I. Recite the last paragraph of the text.

II. Decide which of the following best states the main idea of the passage.

A. The wise use of leisure time has become an important problem for everyone.

B. Today, working less than 40 hours a week, people enjoy more leisure time.

C. However short the work week becomes, work is still the most important part of life.

D. Leisure and recreation go together, though they are not necessarily the same thing.

III. Answer the following questions.

1. How many hours did the average factory worker labor a week in 1840? What does "from can to can't " mean in the first pragraph?

2. Why is it a particularly difficult problem for the sick, the aged, and the retired to use leisure time wisely?

3. How does the author look at work and leisure?

4. What is the relationship between leisure and recreation, according to your understanding?

=== **VOCABULARY AND STRUCTURE** ===

I. Match words or phrases in Column A with their explanations in Column B.

A	B
1. privilege	a. free time, spare time
2. enjoy	b. a special advantage
3. hence	c. mean, an intermediate level or degree
4. average	d. to receive pleasure or satisfaction from; like
5. contribute to	e. therefore
6. particular	f. to stop working
7. depend on	g. to make a contribution to
8. worthwhile	h. important to be worth one's time, effort, or interest
9. retire	i. to rely on
10. leisure time	j. special

II. Fill in the blank in each sentence with a word or phrase taken from the box below. Change the word form if necessary.

earn one's living	particularly	retire	worthwhile
contribute to	go maintain	lead	

1. I _____ like the brown shoes.

2. Gossip and lying _____ together.

3. It is not easy for anyone to _____ if he doesn't have any skills.

4. You can _____ at 60.

5. It is _____ making such an experiment.

6. Exercise _____ better health.

III. *Rewrite the following sentences after the model.*

Model

Those people have much leisure.   It's hard for them to find interesting and worthwhile ways to use it.

Those people have *so* much leisure *that* it is hard for them to find interesting and worthwhile ways to use it.

1. The teacher is very wonderful. He is quite popular with all his students.

   _____.

2. The weather was very hot. All the children went swimming the whole afternoon.

   _____.

We use leisure wisely. Work itself can become rewarding and enjoyable.

We use leisure wisely *so that* work itself can become rewarding and enjoyable.

3. The little boy saved every coin. He could buy his mother a present on Mother's day.

   _____.

4. Please speak loudly. Your classmates can hear you clearly.

   _____.

IV. *Translate the following sentences into Chinese.*

1. It is a particularly difficult problem for the sick, the aged, and those who have retired from earning a living.

2. We do not work to get leisure and the pleasures leisure brings us; rather, we use leisure wisely so that work itself can become rewarding and enjoyable.

3. When one speaks of making good use of leisure, he means choosing recreational activities, which contribute to health, growth, and spirit.

V. Translate the following sentences with words or phrases learnt in Text A.

1. 你们国家八月份的平均（average）降雨量（rainfall）是多少？

2. 这电影值得一看。（It is worthwhile…）

3. 他的一家人全靠他养活。（depend on）

4. 啤酒与奶酪一起吃味道很好。（go together）

5. 我们要很好地利用时间。（make use of）

 **Speaking**

I. How to Ask the Time

Some "DO's" in Asking the Time

There are many different ways to ask the time. It's high time we talked about the time! Here are some "do's" in reading the time first.

☺ Simply read the hours and the minute.

Have a go at these: 7:30, 9:45, 11:15, and 12:20.

No problem. Eh? Seven thirty, nine forty-five, eleven fifteen, twelve twenty. Can you say these times in a more 'usual' way? That's right! Half past seven, a quarter to ten, a quarter past eleven, twenty past twelve.

☺ For five, ten, twenty, twenty-five minutes past the hour you may leave out "minutes", for all the other minutes past the hour, it is better to put the word in!

Try these: 6:37, 9:52, 11:59, 12:33

The following are the right answers: Twenty-seven minutes past six, eight minutes to ten, one minute/a minute to twelve, twenty-seven minutes to one.

☺ Telling the time in a very modern and very colloquial way is like this: instead of "past" we use "after" and instead of "to" we use "before". e. g.

five after six

thirty after eleven

twenty before four

Useful Sentences	
What day is (it) today? What day of the week is it today?	It's Monday /Tuesday, etc. Today is Tuesday.
What's the date today? What's today's date? What date is it today?	It's January / April 10th. It's May 1st.
What time is it? Time, please? What's the time, please? What time do you make it? What time does your watch say? What's the time now? What time do you have? Could you tell/give me the time? Have you got the time, please? What's the time by your watch?	It's five o'clock /half past (after) five/a quarter to (before) five /five thirty, etc It's 5:30. It's fourteen minutes after/ past five (5:14). It's seven minutes before / to five (4:53).

Model

Asking about the Time

(Michael asks about the time on his way out to work.)

Michael: Honey, can you tell me the time?

Lily: Sure. It's 7:50 by my watch.

Michael: Gosh (糟了)! I'm late for the meeting. No matter what, I won't be able to get to the office within 10 minutes.

Lily: No hurry. I didn't tell you that my watch is 15 minutes fast.

Michael: You scared me! You don't know how hard my boss is.

(Michael asks Lily about the time of her routine life.)

Michael: When do you usually get up?

Lily: I usually get up at about six thirty every morning.

Michael: When does your father go to work?

Lily: He goes to work at about 7:15 every morning. He works in a bank.

Michael: When is the bank open?

Lily: It is open Monday to Friday from eight a. m. until five p. m.

Michael: Then at what time does your father get home from work?

Lily: At about a quarter to six. Today he picks me up at five thirty, because we have an appointment with Professor Jones at six o'clock.

II. Practice

1. Complete the following conversations and then act them out in pairs.

1) Peter and Man Lin went fishing together. They chatted with each other.

Peter: How many fish have you caught, Man Lin?

Man Lin: Five. What _____ you?

Peter: I have _____ fish. I've caught eight.

Man Lin: _____ _____ is it now?

Peter: It's half _____ five.

Man Lin: Oh, it's time _____ supper. Let's go home.

Peter: OK. Let's _____.

2) Grace: Li Jian, _____ is it today?

Li Jian: _____ Wednesday.

Grace: And what's the _____ today?

Li Jian: Er... _____ March 11.

Grace: Oh, it's Tree Planting Day tomorrow.

Li Jian: Yes. _____ we go and plant some trees?

Grace: That's a good idea.

2. Work in pairs. Practice asking the time with your partner according to the situations below. Then switch roles.

1) Peter and Alice are schoolmates in a vocational college. They find they have much more leisure time than they had in senior high school. Now they are talking with each other

about how to spend their leisure time.

2) The winter vacation was just over. The students were quite happy to see each other again and chatted with each other, talking about how they spent the winter vacation.

B Listening

Listen to the conversations and choose the best answer to each of the questions you hear.

1. A. It's Friday.　　　　B. It's December 20th.　　C. It's Christmas Day.

2. A. Alice　　　　　　　B. Wang Yan　　　　　　C. Smith

3. A. Monday, October 6th.　　　　　　B. Saturday, October 1st.

　C. Saturday, October 6th　　　　　　D. Monday, October 1st.

4. A. Oct. 1st.　　B. Oct. 4th.　　C. Oct. 6th.　　D. Oct. 16th.

5. A. John.　　　　　　B. The stranger　　　C. Joan.

6. A. 7:15　　　　　　　B. 7:30　　　　　　　C. 8:30

7. A. 5:30　　　　　　　B. 12:00　　　　　　C. 5:45.

8. A. Peter and Carol seldom go and eat in a Chinese restaurant.

　B. Jane is a friend of Peter's.

　C. Carol likes her school very much.

C Sounds and Spellings

I. Listen and practice. Pay special attention to the pronunciation of the italicized letters.

1. /ɑː/　*car*, h*a*lf, h*ea*rt, l*au*gh, *a*nswer
2. /əu/　g*o*, c*oa*t, s*ou*l, b*ow*l
3. /ɔː/　h*o*rse, s*aw*, *ou*ght, *Au*gust, *a*ll, *o*re, d*oo*r, *oa*r, f*ou*r, w*a*rn
4. /u/　c*oo*k, sh*ou*ld, b*u*ll
5. /uː/　f*oo*d, t*o*mb, fr*ui*t

II. Listen and practice. Pay special attention to the pronunciation of the plosives in continuous speech.

1. A bargain is a bargain.　达成的协议不可撕毁。

2. A fault confessed is half redressed.　浪子回头金不换。

3. A flow of words is no proof of wisdom.　口若悬河不能作为才智的证明。

4. A good book is a light to the soul.　好书一本,照亮心灵。

5. All that glitters is not gold.　闪光的东西并不都是金子。

III. Read and enjoy.

Riddles

1. What follows a horse wherever he goes?

2. What kind of dog has no tail

3. What is faster, heat or cold?

☺☺☺☺☺

1. His tail.　2. A hot dog.　3. Heat. Because you can catch a cold.

Answers:

 **Grammar**

I. Fill in the blanks with the words given in brackets and change the word form when necessary.

1. Which is _____ (big), the sun, the moon or the Earth?

2. Which is _____ (beautiful), the black coat or the blue one?

3. This moon-cake is _____ (cheap) of all.

4. He is the _____ (strong) in the class.

5. He drives much _____ (care) than he did three years ago.

6. "How was the old man this morning?" "He looked _____. (happy)"

7. The _____ (hard) you work, the _____ (great) progress you will make.

8. Travelling is _____ (excite), but we often feel _____ (tire) when we are back from travels.

9. It's summer now. The weather is getting _____ and _____. (hot)

10. I will come back as _____ (quick) as possible.

II. Choose the one that best completes the sentence from the four choices marked A, B, C and D below each sentence.

1. Bob never does his homework _____ Mary. He makes lots of mistakes.

   A. so careful as   B. as carefully as   C. carefully as   D. as careful as

2. Now air in our town is _____ than it used to be. Something must be done about it.

   A. very good   B. much better   C. rather than   D. even worse

3. I feel _____ better than yesterday.

   A. more   B. very   C. the   D. far

4. China has a larger population than _____ in the world.

   A. all the countries   B. every country   C. any country   D. any other country

5. This book is _____ on the subject.

   A. the much best   B. much the best   C. very much best   D. very the best

6. The sick boy is getting _____ day by day.

   A. worse   B. bad   C. badly   D. worst

7. This necklace looks _____ and sells _____.

   A. well, well   B. good, nice   C. nice, good   D. nice, well

8. Doctor Wang _____ heart operations.

   A. is interested on   B. like doing   C. does well in   D. do good in

9. I liked to play football when I was young. _____.

   A. So he was   B. So was he   C. So did he   D. So he did

10. I didn't go shopping yesterday. He didn't _____.

   A. so   B. either   C. too   D. neither

Writing

I. General Writing

Read the following passage as part of an article for the local paper on how the local people spend their leisure time and then write a short paragraph about how college students spend their leisure time.

People who work indoors and spend most of their time sitting and doing sedentary (需长坐的) office work can add physical activity to their lives by doing sports during their leisure

time, such as playing a ball game, going camping, hiking or fishing. On the other hand, people whose jobs involve a lot of physical activity may prefer to spend their free time doing quiet, relaxing activities, such as reading books or magazines or watching TV. Some people find that collecting stamps, postcards, badges, model cars or ships, bottles, or antiques is a relaxing hobby.

II. Writing for Specific Purposes

Read the following sample and then write an invitation card to one of your friends. It can be a card for a holiday, birthday, anniversary or any other occasions.

Invitation Cards

Generally speaking, there are formal invitations and informal invitations. A formal invitation usually includes the following key information: the inviter's name, the occasion or the reason of this invitation, the invitee's name, the date, time, and location.

An informal invitation letter should also include the above-mentioned information. But the format is much simpler, the language is rather informal, and the invitation can be given by common letters, notes, or telephone calls.

Here are some samples of invitation and the reply. You can follow them to produce one of yours.

> Ms. Maggie A. Green
> requests the pleasure of
> Salim A Dabougi's
> company at a dinner
> on Friday, the sixth of September
> at 7:00 pm
> at Maxim's No. 88, Chongwenmen Street
> Beijing
> For Regrets Only   Lounge Suits

It is a more polite way to write the reply in a handwritten form.

> Mr. Salim A Dabougi
> accepts with pleasure
> the kind invitation
> of
> Ms. Maggie A. Green
> to be present at dinner
> on Friday, the sixth of September
> at 7:30 pm
> at Maxim's No. 88, Chongwenmen Street
> Beijing

An invitation can also be made in the form of a letter, both formal and casual. Here are some samples.

 ## Sample

Dear Mr. Johns,

We are pleased to inform you that an important exhibition of our latest products will be held at the International Exposition Center in Beijing from October 12 to October 20, 2002.

You will find several new designs that might be of interest to you. Furthermore, you might also find interesting the improvements on several of our earlier products.

We are looking forward to your visit at our booth, namely, booth 89 in Exhibition Hall No. 10.

Yours sincerely,

Zhang Yi

 Sample

Dear Zhang Wei,

    I am going to hold my birthday party at our apartment on Saturday, August 31, at 7.00 p.m. Would you and Lee like to come over?

Yours,

Peter Jackson

TEXT B   How Do the British Spend Their Leisure Time?

    According to our **interviews** in Leeds City Center, Britain's most common leisure activities are home-**based** or **social**; but they are different in different time periods.

    1. **Weekdays** after work: Weekdays after work is not so long a time for people to have much to do, and most people think they are very **tired** after work and what they really need is time to have a rest. Most British we interviewed like to stay at home, watch television and **videos**, listen to the radio, do sports, **surf** the **net**, play **e-games**, and read some books. So these activities are by far the most **popular** leisure **pastimes**.

    Of course there are more activities than those **mentioned** above. Some young men like to go to **pubs**, **theaters**, cinemas, **parties**, **coffee bars**, and **clubs** after work.

    2. Weekends: "Weekends are the days I am looking forward to;" said Linda F., "I can do shopping, especially choose some beautiful clothes, I can **meet** my friends and go to the pub, theater, cinema, parties, coffee bars, clubs, etc. I also will visit my parents or my **relatives**, and if the weather is fine, I may go out with my family." That was **possibly** what we heard during our interviews. Some men said that they worked in their gardens; they made something by themselves, such as **painting** walls, making some **stools**, or **building** something in their gardens. They called these activities DIY.

3. Holidays: Holidays are the best time to **arrange** leisure activities, because in Britain there are five weeks' paid holiday **per year** (workers gained the **right** in 1981). "If the holiday is long, I like to spend my holidays **abroad**", said a teacher in LMU, "and if it is not long enough, I shall plan some **trips** to nearby **areas**. I love to be in **nature** and I also love to see different **countries**." Of course there are many other answers: some like to stay at home, watching TV; some like to visit their relatives.

(335 words)

New Words

spend	/spend/	v.	度过;花费
interview	/ˈɪntəvjuː/	n.	采访 v. 接见;会见;(记者的)访问
base	/beɪs/	v.	以…作基础,基于… n. 基础,根据地
social	/ˈsəʊʃl/	a.	社会的,社交的,群居的
weekday	/ˈwiːkdeɪ/	n.	工作日,平日
tired	/ˈtaɪəd/	a.	疲劳的,累的,疲倦的
★video	/ˈvɪdiəʊ/	n.	电视,录像,视频
▲surf	/sɜːf/	v.	在…冲浪;作冲浪运动
net	/net/	n.	网,网络
▲e-game	/iːgeɪm/	n.	电子游戏
popular	/ˈpɒpjələ/	a.	流行的,受欢迎的
★pastime	/ˈpɑːstaɪm/	n.	消遣,娱乐
mention	/ˈmenʃn/	v.	提及,说起
▲pub	/pʌb/	n.	小酒馆
theater	/ˈθɪətə/	n.	剧场,戏院,电影院
party	/ˈpɑːti/	n.	集会,聚会,宴会等
coffee	/ˈkɒfi/	n.	咖啡
bar	/bɑː/	n.	吧台,酒吧间
club	/klʌb/	n.	俱乐部,夜总会
meet	/miːt/	v.	(赴约)和…会面,遇见
relative	/ˈrelətɪv/	n.	亲戚 a. 有关系的

possibly	/ˈpɒsəbli/	*ad.*	可能,或者
paint	/peɪnt/	*v.*	油漆　*n.* 油漆,颜料
▲ stool	/stuːl/	*n.*	凳子
build	/bɪld/	*v.*	建造,建筑
arrange	/əˈreɪndʒ/	*v.*	安排,准备
per	/pə/	*prep.*	每,每一
right	/raɪt/	*n.*	权利,正义,右边　*a.* 正当的,正确的
abroad	/əˈbrɔːd/	*ad.*	在国外,到海外
trip	/trɪp/	*n.*	(短途)旅行　*v.* 旅行,远足
area	/ˈeərɪə/	*n.*	地区,区域
nature	/ˈneɪtʃə/	*n.*	自然,大自然,自然界
country	/ˈkʌntri/	*n.*	国家,国土

Phrases and Expressions

according to	按照;根据…所说
have a rest	休息
by far	最,显然;达到极为明显的程度
look forward to	期望;期待,盼望
coffee bar	咖啡馆
by oneself	单独,独自
DIY (*abbr.* Do It Yourself)	自己动手做

Proper Names

Leeds City Center　　　　　　　利兹[英格兰北部城市]市中心
LMU (Leeds Metropolitan University) 利兹都市大学（英国最大、最受欢迎的大学之一）

课文词数	生词总量	生词比率	二级词汇	三级词汇	超纲词汇
335	40	11.9%	34	2	4

Judge , according to the text , whether the following statements are True or False.

1. _____ According the passage, Britain's most common leisure activities are home-based and social.

2. _____ Most British think they are very tired after work and what they really need is time to have a rest.

3. _____ Activities at home are by far the most popular leisure pastimes for most British.

4. _____ Activities like going to the pub, theater, cinema, parties, coffee bars, clubs etc. are called DIY.

5. _____ The best time to arrange leisure activities is holidays, because in Britain there is a five-week unpaid holiday per year.

Unit 8 Internet

TEXT A   The Internet

As we approach a new **millennium**, the **Internet** is **revolutionizing** our society, our **economy** and our **technological** systems. No one knows for **certain** how far, or in what **direction**, the Internet will develop. But no one should **underestimate** its importance.

Over the past century and a half, important technological **developments** have created a **global** environment that is drawing the people of the world closer and closer together. During the **industrial revolution**, we learned to put motors to work to **magnify** human and animal **muscle** power. In the new **Information** Age, we are learning to magnify **brainpower** by putting the power of **computation** wherever we need it, and to provide information services on a global basis. The Internet, as an **integrating** force, has **melded** the **technology** of communications and **computing** to provide **instant connection** and global information services to all its users at very low cost.

Ten years ago, most of the world knew little or nothing about the Internet. It was the **private enclave** of computer **scientists** and researchers who used it to **interact** with **colleagues** in their **respective disciplines**. Today, the Internet's **magnitude** is thousands of times what it was only a **decade** ago. It is **estimated** that about 60 **million host** computers on the Internet today **serve** about 200 million users in over 200 countries and **territories**. Today's telephone system is still much larger: about 3 **billion** people around the world now talk on almost 950 million telephone **lines** (about 250 million of which are actually radio-based **cell phones**). But by the end of the year 2000, people estimate there will be at least 300 million Internet users. Also, the total numbers of host computers and users have been growing at about 33% every six months since 1988 — or **roughly** 80% per year. The telephone service, in **comparison**, grows an **average** of about 5%-10% per year.

(309 words)

New Words

Internet	/ˈɪntənet/	*n.*	互联网;英特网
millennium	/mɪˈleniəm/	*n.*	千年期(尤指公元纪年);千禧年
▲revolutionize	/ˌrevəˈluːʃənaɪz/	*v.*	完全变革;彻底改变
economy	/ɪˈkɒnəmi/	*n.*	经济情况;经济
★technological	/ˌteknəˈlɒdʒɪkl/	*a.*	科技的
certain	/ˈsɜːtn/	*a.*	确定;肯定
direction	/dəˈrekʃn/	*n.*	方向;方位
★underestimate	/ˌʌndərˈestɪmeɪt/	*v.*	低估;轻视
development	/dɪˈveləpmənt/	*n.*	发展;壮大
★global	/ˈgləʊbl/	*a.*	全球的;全世界的
industrial	/ɪnˈdʌstriəl/	*a.*	工业的;产业的
revolution	/ˌrevəˈluːʃn/	*n.*	大变革;革命
★magnify	/ˈmæɡnɪfaɪ/	*v.*	增强;放大
muscle	/ˈmʌsl/	*n.*	肌肉;体力
information	/ˌɪnfəˈmeɪʃn/	*n.*	信息;消息
▲brainpower	/ˈbreɪnpaʊə/	*n.*	智力;智能
computation	/ˌkɒmpjuˈteɪʃn/	*n.*	计算;计算过程
★integrate	/ˈɪntɪɡreɪt/	*v.*	成为一体;(使)加入
▲meld	/meld/	*v.*	结合;融合
★technology	/tekˈnɒlədʒi/	*n.*	科技;工艺
compute	/kəmˈpjuːt/	*v.*	计算;估算
★instant	/ˈɪnstənt/	*a.*	立即的;立刻的 *n.* 瞬间;片刻
connection	/kəˈnekʃn/	*n.*	连接;联系
private	/ˈpraɪvət/	*a.*	私人的;私立的
▲enclave	/ˈenkleɪv/	*n.*	飞地(某国或某市境内隶属外国或外市,具有不同宗教、文化或民族的领土)

scientist	/ˈsaɪəntɪst/	n.	科学家
interact	/ˌɪntərˈækt/	v.	交流；相互影响
★colleague	/ˈkɒliːɡ/	n.	同事；同僚
★respective	/rɪˈspektɪv/	a.	各自的；分别的
★discipline	/ˈdɪsəplɪn/	n.	知识领域；行为准则　　v. 自我控制；严格要求
▲magnitude	/ˈmæɡnɪtjuːd/	n.	重要性；巨大
★decade	/ˈdekeɪd/	n.	十年期(尤指一个年代)；十年
★estimate	/ˈestɪmət/	v.	估计；估算　　n. 估计；估价
million	/ˈmɪljən/	num.	百万
host	/həʊst/	n.	主机；主人　　v. 主办；做东
serve	/sɜːv/	v.	能满足…的需要，供应
★territory	/ˈterətri/	n.	地区；领土
▲billion	/ˈbɪljən/	num.	十亿
line	/laɪn/	n.	电话线路；线条　　v. 沿…形成行；(用…)做衬里
cell	/sel/	n.	(大结构中的)小隔室(如蜂房巢室)；细胞
phone	/fəʊn/	n.	电话；电话机　　v. 打电话
roughly	/ˈrʌfli/	ad.	大约；差不多
comparison	/kəmˈpærɪsn/	n.	比较；相比
average	/ˈævərɪdʒ/	n.	平均数　　a. 平均的；普通的

Phrases and Expressions

interact with	交流；相互影响
It is estimated that…	据估计…
at least	至少；不少于
in comparison	(与…)相比较

Proper Names

| Information Age | 信息时代 |

课文词数	生词总量	生词比率	二级词汇	三级词汇	超纲词汇
309	44	14%	25	13	6

GETTING THE MESSAGE

I. *Recite the second paragraph of the text.*

II. *Decide which of the following best states the main idea of the passage.*

    A. No one knows how far the Internet will develop.

    B. The importance of the Internet in our life.

    C. The history of telephone.

    D. How does the Internet revolutionize our life during the industrial revolution?

III. *Answer the following questions.*

    1. When did the Internet begin to revolutionize our society, economy and technological systems?

    2. Does anyone know how far, or in what direction, the Internet will develop?

    3. How does the Internet provide instant connection and global information services to its users?

    4. Some people say that computers will take the place of television in our life in the near future. Do you agree? Why?

VOCABULARY AND STRUCTURE

I. *Match words or phrases in Column A with their explanations in Column B.*

A	B
1. computation	a. a period of 1,000 years
2. interact	b. the general position a person or thing moves or points towards
3. private	c. covering or affecting the whole world
4. serve	d. a great change in conditions, ways of working, beliefs, etc. that affects large numbers of people
5. millennium	e. an act or the process of calculating something
6. revolution	f. belonging to or for the use of a particular person or group
7. phone	g. to communicate with somebody, especially while you work, play or spend time with them

(Continued)

8. direction	h. to be useful to somebody in achieving or satisfying something
9. average	i. a system for talking to somebody else over long distances using wires or radio
10. global	j. the result of adding several amounts together, finding a total, and dividing the total by the number of amounts

II. Fill in the blanks in each sentence with a word or phrase taken from the box below. Change the word form if necessary.

approach	develop	provide	instant
information	serve	economy	host

1. Lucy studies _____ at college.

2. China is a _____ country.

3. This bookstore _____ all kinds of books.

4. Eating too much _____ food is bad for health.

5. As you _____ the town, you'll see a red building on the right.

6. Nowadays we can get more _____ from the Internet.

III. Rewrite the following sentences after the model.

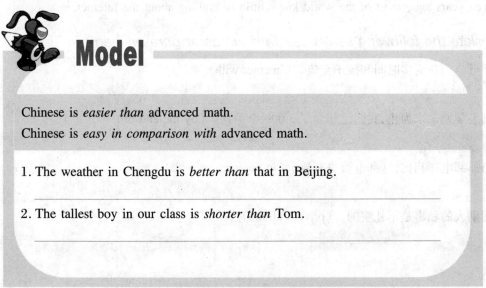

Model

Chinese is *easier than* advanced math.
Chinese is *easy in comparison with* advanced math.

1. The weather in Chengdu is *better than* that in Beijing.

_____

2. The tallest boy in our class is *shorter than* Tom.

_____

Model

People *estimate* by the end of the year 2000 there will be at least 300 million Internet users.

It is estimated that by the end of the year 2000 there will be at least 300 million Internet users.

3. People *estimate* the increase of the population will be slower and slower.

_____

4. People *estimate* computers will be cheaper in the future.

_____

IV. Translate the following sentences into Chinese.

1. As we approach a new millennium, the Internet is revolutionizing our society, our economy and our technological systems.

2. During the industrial revolution, we learned to put motors to work to magnify human and animal muscle power.

3. Ten years ago, most of the world knew little or nothing about the Internet.

V. Translate the following sentences with words or phrases learnt in Text A.

1. 父母应当花更多时间和孩子交流。(interact with)

2. 到上学期期末为止，我们已经学了 5 000 个单词。(by the end of)

3. 与那部电影相比，这部电影更有趣。(in comparison with)

4. 问别人的私事是不礼貌的。(private affairs)

 **Speaking**

I. How to Talk About the Weather

Why do the English Talk about the Weather?

Foreigners are surprised that the English-speaking spend so much time discussing the weather. The reason for this is not simply that their weather is interesting and variable, but that the English-speaking are unwilling to talk about personal matters with people who are not friends. Mentioning the weather can be a useful and inoffensive(不冒犯的) way of starting a conversation with a stranger at a party or in a railway station.

Useful Sentences	
How's the weather? What's the weather like?	It's rainy/ cloudy/windy/foggy. It's sunny/snowy/drizzly(毛毛细雨的).
Nice day today, isn't it? How nice it is here!	Yes, it is. It certainly is.
How long will this weather last? It seems to be warmer/colder/clearing up. They say we're in for drizzle/rain/snow. It never rains/drizzles/snows all the year, does it? We have four seasons of spring, summer, autumn and winter. The sun/the breeze is shinning/blowing.	They say it's going to rain tomorrow. I don't know. I hope it will stay fine. Apparently it's going to turn colder / warmer. I don't mind as long as it doesn't snow/ rain. No, it doesn't. (对,不下。) Yes, it does. (不,下雨/下小雨/下雪。) It must be easy to see a rainbow(彩虹) after the rain.

Model

Jane：It seems to be clearing up.

John：It makes a change, doesn't it?

Jane：Apparently it's going to turn warmer.

John：But they say we're in for drizzle next week.

Jane：I don't mind as long as it doesn't snow.

John：It's impossible. The spring's coming.

Jane：Let's hope it gets warmer soon.

John：As long as it is not too hot.

Li Lei：Nice day today, isn't it?

Lucy： Yes, it's beautiful weather we are having.

Li Lei：We can't complain about the weather recently.

Lucy： Yes, it's neither too hot nor too cold.

Li Lei：I wonder how long it will last?

Lucy： They say it's going to rain tomorrow.

Li Lei：Really? I planned to have a picnic with my family.

Lucy： Oh, maybe you have to wait another day.

II. Practice

1. Complete the following conversations and then act them out in pairs.

1) Kerry and Shelley are spending their holiday in Sanya.

Kerry： _____ it is here.

Shelley：It certainly is. The sun is _____ but there's a pleasant _____ . It's lovely.

Kerry： I've heard the weather here is ideal, just like spring most of the year.

Shelley：That's just like Dali, my hometown. We have _____ .

Kerry： It never rains or _____ all the year, does it?

Shelley：Yes, It does rain, but only a little.

Kerry： It must be easy to see the _____ after the rain?

Shelley：It's as plain as the nose on your face.

2) The woman and the man are talking about the weather.

Woman：What a cold _____ today!

Man: Yes, it _____. It is snowing now.

Woman: Really?

Man: Yes, it is the first snow this year. _____ make a snowman together.

Woman: _____. Let's go.

2. Work in pairs. Practise talking about the weather with your partner according to the situations below. Then switch roles.

1) Wu Mei, a freshman of Sichuan Normal University, goes back to her hometown Sanya, Hainan in January. Now her mother is talking about the weather with her.

2) Li Lei is inviting Lucy to have a picnic. But it has been reported that the weather will not be very good.

B Listening

Listen to the four conversations and choose the best answer to each of the questions you hear.

1. A. Cloudy.   B. Snowy.   C. Sunny.

2. A. They plan to put on overcoat and gloves.

   B. They plan to go upstairs.

   C. They plan to go outside and make a snowman.

3. A. At a party.   B. In a bank.   C. In a school.

4. A. Windy.   B. Rainy.   C. Sunny.

5. A. Rainy.   B. Cloudy.   C. Sunny.

6. A. From twelve to sixteen.

   B. From fifteen to twenty.

   C. From twenty to twenty-four.

7. A. He means it's cool in the classroom.

   B. He means it's boring in the classroom.

   C. He means it's very hot in the classroom.

8. A. A drought.   B. A flood.   C. An earthquake.

Sounds and Spellings

I. Listen and practise. Pay special attention to the pronunciation of the italicized letters.

1. /eɪ/ c*a*ke, st*ai*n, b*ay*, w*ei*ght, conv*ey*, st*ea*k

2. /aɪ/ p*i*lot, sk*y*, p*ie*, d*ye*, *ei*ther, n*igh*t, Th*ai*land

3. /ɔɪ/ *oi*l, b*oy*

4. /ɪə/ d*ear*, b*eer*, h*ere*, front*ier*, souven*ir*, th*ea*ter, med*ia*, th*eo*ry

5. /eə/ h*are*, f*air*, t*ear*

6. /ʊə/ p*oor*, t*our*, s*ure*, cr*ue*l, us*ua*l, r*ura*l

7. /aʊ/ ar*ou*nd, c*ow*

8. /əʊ/ sm*o*ke, c*oa*t, t*oe*, s*ou*l, bl*ow*

II. Listen and practise. Pay special attention to the pronunciation of the plosives in continuous speech.

1. Ma*k*e ha*y* whi*l*e the sun sh*i*nes.　趁热打铁。

2. N*o* j*oy* with*ou*t ann*oy*. 喜中有忧。

3. If there be n*ei*ther sn*ow* nor r*ai*n, then will be d*ear* all sorts of gr*ai*n.
　雨雪不调，五谷价高。

4. Prep*are* for a r*ai*ny d*ay*. 未雨绸缪。

5. P*oor* men's words have little w*eigh*t. 人微言轻。

III. Read and enjoy.

1. A loyal warrior will rarely worry why we rule.
2. A noise annoys an oyster, but a noisy noise annoys an oyster more!
3. The great Greek grape growers grow great Greek grapes.
4. A writer named Wright was instructing his little son how to write Wright right.

   He said: "It is not right to write Wright as 'rite'. Try to write Wright aright!"

   ☺☺☺☺☺

 Grammar

I. Fill in the blanks with the words given and change the form of words when necessary.

1. Tom's father _____ an engineer. (be)

2. I _____ interested in playing Ping-Pong. (be)

3. I _____ reading the English book at 8:00 last night. (be)

4. _____ you finished reading the novels? No, I _____. (have)

5. They _____ go to see their grandfather tomorrow. (will)

6. I'll _____ having a meeting at 12 tomorrow. (be)

7. _____ speak to your father like that. (do not)

8. Li Lei _____ like swimming. (do not)

9. I _____ see him at the party last night. (do not)

10. I _____ told him to drive slowly, but he didn't take my advice. (have)

II. Choose the one that best completes the sentence from the four choices marked A, B, C and D below each sentence.

1. They _____ to start training next Friday.

   A. be   B. are

   C. is   D. will

2. The children _____ the cake up before Lucy came back.

   A. had eaten   B. have eaten

   C. has eaten   D. have ate

3. He _____ been reading in the library since 9:00 this morning.

    A. have   B. had

    C. has   D. is

4. We _____ all the work tomorrow.

    A. shall have finished   B. shall finished

    C. have finished   D. finish

5. He _____ tell me that he would help hus clean the house.

    A. do   B. does

    C. did   D. done

6. What _____ you like to drink?

    A. will   B. shall

    C. would   D. did

7. He told me he _____ help me with my English.

    A. will   B. should

    C. doesn't   D. would

8. If I had studied hard, I _____ have passed the exam.

    A. will   B. would

    C. shall   D. /

9. If I were you, I _____ forgive him.

    A. will   B. would

    C. didn't   D. don't

10. I _____ cook now. My mother will come back for lunch.

    A. have to   B. having

    C. having to   D. /

Writing

General Writing

With the development of technology, surfing on the Internet is as plain as the nose on your face. Various websites provide different services for us daily. The following are two useful websites.

    1) http://www. sina. com. cn It is an all-around website. It provides services in e-mail, news, investment, reading etc.

    2) http://www. verycd. com It is a professional downloading website. It offers plenty of movies, songs and study materials. What's more, all services are free.

    Read the following passage and then write a short introduction for a website. You are

required to read it aloud in class next time.

Sample

Good morning, everyone. Today I'd like to recommend a good website for you. The website is http://www. dangdang. com. It is a professional online bookshop. It offers various services on ordering and mailing books. With its help, you can enjoy shopping for books at home. Now, Dangdang. com has developed other services on the Internet. If you want to get more information, just click the above website.

TEXT B — The History of the Internet

Many people think that the Internet is a **recent innovation**, when in fact the **essence** of it has been around for over a **quarter** century. The Internet began as ARPAnet, a U. S. Department of **Defense projects** to create a nationwide computer network that would continue to function even if a large **portion** of it were **destroyed** in a **nuclear** war or natural disaster.

During the next two decades, the network that **evolved** was used **primarily** by **academic institutions**, scientists and the government for research and communications. The **appeal** of the Internet to these bodies was obvious, as it allowed **disparate** institutions to connect to each others' computing systems and **databases**, as well as share data **via E-mail**.

The nature of the Internet changed **abruptly** in 1992, when the U. S. government began pulling out of network **management**, and **commercial entities** offered Internet access to the general public for the first time. This change in focus **marked** the beginning of the Internet's **astonishing expansion**.

According to a **survey conducted** by **Commerce**Net and Nielsen **Media** Research in early 1997, nearly one out of every four Americans over the age of 16 is an Internet user. And the number of users worldwide is believed to be well into the tens of millions. Other **statistics** are **equally startling**:

A CNN report stated that Internet **traffic** in 1996 was 25 times what it was just two years earlier.

The market research group IntelliQuest **pegged** the number of Internet users in the U. S. in late 1996 at 47 million.

The technology research firm IDG estimates that by century's end, *one billion people* worldwide will have access to personal computers — more than doubling the computer-**savvy** population of 1996.

The Internet **explosion coincides** with the **advent** of **increasingly** powerful yet **reasonably** priced personal computers with easy-to-use **graphical operating** systems. The result has been an **attraction** of recent computer "**converts**" to the network, and new **possibilities** for **exploiting** a **wealth** of **multimedia capabilities**.

(328 words)

New Words

recent	/ˈriːsnt/	*a.*	新近的；近来的
▲innovation	/ˌɪnəˈveɪʃn/	*n.*	创新；新思想(或方法)
★essence	/ˈesns/	*n.*	实质；精髓
quarter	/ˈkwɔːtə/	*n.*	四分之一；15 分钟
defense	/dɪˈfens/	*n.*	国防机构；防御
project	/prəˈdʒekt/	*v.*	规划；计划
	/ˈprɒdʒekt/	*n.*	方案；项目
★portion	/ˈpɔːʃn/	*n.*	部分；一份
destroy	/dɪˈstrɔɪ/	*v.*	破坏；摧毁
nuclear	/ˈnjuːklɪə/	*a.*	核武器的；原子能的
▲evolve	/iˈvɒlv/	*v.*	逐步发展；进化
primarily	/praɪˈmerəli/	*ad.*	主要地；根本地
academic	/ˌækəˈdemɪk/	*a.*	学术的；学业的
institution	/ˌɪnstɪˈtjuːʃn/	*n.*	机构；社会福利机构
★appeal	/əˈpiːl/	*n.*	魅力；上诉 *v.* 上诉；有吸引力
▲disparate	/ˈdɪspərət/	*a.*	由不同的人(或事物)组成的；炯然不同的
database	/ˈdeɪtəbeɪs/	*n.*	数据库；资料库
★via	/ˈvaɪə/	*prep.*	通过；经由

e-mail	/ˈiːmeɪl/	n.	电子邮件
▲abruptly	/əˈbrʌptli/	ad.	突然地；意外地
management	/ˈmænɪdʒmənt/	n.	管理；管理部门
★commercial	/kəˈmɜːʃl/	a.	商业性的；商业化的　　n. 广告
▲entity	/ˈentəti/	n.	实体；独立存在物
mark	/mɑːk/	v.	成为…的征兆；做记号　　n. 符号；标志
astonishing	/əˈstɒnɪʃɪŋ/	a.	难以置信的；令人十分惊讶的
★expansion	/ɪkˈspænʃn/	n.	膨胀；扩展
survey	/ˈsɜːveɪ/	n.	民意调查；勘测
	/səˈveɪ/	v.	（对…）作民意调查；查看
conduct	/kənˈdʌkt/	v.	组织；安排
	/ˈkɒndʌkt/	n.	行为；举止
★commerce	/ˈkɒmɜːs/	n.	商务；贸易
media	/ˈmiːdiə/	n.	大众传播媒介
★statistic	/stəˈtɪstɪk/	n.	(pl.)统计数字；统计资料
equally	/ˈiːkwəli/	ad.	同样地；相等地
▲startling	/ˈstɑːtlɪŋ/	a.	让人震惊的；惊人的
★traffic	/ˈtræfɪk/	n.	交通；货流
▲peg	/peg/	v.	使工资、价格固定于某水平；用夹子夹住
		n.	楔子；短桩
▲savvy	/ˈsævi/	n.	了解；实际知识　　a. 有见识的；通情达理的
explosion	/ɪkˈspləʊʒn/	n.	激增；爆炸
▲coincide	/ˌkəʊɪnˈsaɪd/	v.	同时发生；相同
▲advent	/ˈædvent/	n.	（重要事件、人物、发明等的）出现
increasingly	/ɪnˈkriːsɪŋli/	ad.	越来越多地；不断增加地
reasonably	/ˈriːznəbli/	ad.	适度地；合乎逻辑地
★graphical	/ˈgræfɪkl/	a.	形象的；绘画的
operate	/ˈɒpəreɪt/	v.	操作；经营
attraction	/əˈtrækʃn/	n.	有吸引力的特征(或品质、人)；有吸引力的事
★convert	/ˈkɒnvɜːt/	n.	改变观点(或信仰)的人
	/kənˈvɜːt/	v.	转换；改变(观点、习惯等)
possibility	/ˌpɒsəˈbɪləti/	n.	机会；可能性
★exploit	/ɪkˈsplɔɪt/	v.	开发；利用
★wealth	/welθ/	n.	丰富；钱财
multimedia	/ˌmʌltiˈmiːdiə/	a.	多媒体的；使用多媒体的
capability	/ˌkeɪpəˈbɪləti/	n.	能力；才能

Phrases and Expressions

in fact	确切地说;事实上
as well as	也;还
pull out of	退出;脱离

Proper Names

ARPAnet	阿帕网(美国国防部高级计划局网络。它被公认为是世界上第一个采用分组交换技术组建的网络。)
Department of Defense	国防部
Nielsen Media Research	尼尔森媒体研究(全球领先的市场研究及媒体资讯公司)
CNN	有线电视新闻网(美国一广播公司)
IDG	美国国际数据集团(全美三大媒体集团之一)

课文词数	生词总量	生词比率	二级词汇	三级词汇	超纲词汇
328	49	15%	26	13	10

Judge, according to the text, whether the following statements are True or False.

1. _____ Few people think that the Internet is a new innovation, when in fact the essence of it has been around for over 25 years.

2. _____ The U. S. government had planned ARPAnet as an international computer network.

3. _____ During the next 20 years, the evolved network made it possible for different institutions to share data by e-mail.

4. _____ Before the year of 1992, the network was mainly managed by the U. S. government.

5. _____ According to a survey in early 1997, all Internet users were at the age of 16.

Vocabulary

A

B

C

D

E

effectively	4A	especially	1A
▲e-game	7B	★essence	8B
element	5A	★essential	4A
e-mail	8B	★essentially	2A
emotion	1B	establish	6A
enable	4B	★estimate	8A
▲enclave	8A	even	5A
★encounter	4A	event	3B
encourage	2B	★eventually	4A
end	2A	▲evolve	8B
energy	7A	example	3A
engineer	6B	except	6B
enjoyable	7A	★executive	5B
enjoy	7A	exercise	3A
▲enroll	2B	★expansion	8B
enthusiastic	6A	experience	2A
▲entity	8B	★exploit	8B
environment	1A	explosion	8B
equally	8B	extent	4A
error	1B		

factory	7A	find	2B
failure	4A	firm	5B
favorable	4A	follow	3B
favorite	2A	▲foremost	4A
▲feat	4A	freedom	5A
feature	3A	friendship	5A
feel	3A	fuel	6B
feeling	7A	fulfill	4A
festival	6A	full	3A
figure	2A	furthermore	4A
★financial	1A		

G

gain	2A	goal	6A
▲gambler	4B	▲goodness	5B
game	6A	graduate	2A
★gene	3A	★graphical	8B
general	1A	grateful	3B
get	3B	grow	2A
★global	8A	▲grudge	5B

H

hang	5A	hit	3B
height	3A	hobby	5A
★hence	7A	honest	5A
▲heritage	5B	honesty	5A
hesitate	4A	host	8A
highway	2B		

I

★identify	5B	indicate	1B
ignore	4B	industrial	8A
imagine	4A	▲industrious	4A
immediately	1A	★inevitable	4A
importance	4A	influence	4B
importantly	2A	information	8A
improve	1B	▲ingredient	4B
improvement	1B	▲innovation	8B
★inappropriate	1A	★instant	8A
inch	3A	institution	8B
★incline	4A	★integrate	8A
income	1A	▲integrity	5A
increasingly	8B	interact	8A
▲indefinitely	3B	interaction	5B
independence	2A	interest	2A

N

O

P

Q

R

race	6B	religion	1A
rare	4B	rely	5A
realistic	1B	remember	1B
realize	5B	require	1B
really	2A	research	1B
reason	6A	research	5B
reasonably	8B	researcher	4B
receive	6A	resemblance	5A
recent	7A	★respective	8A
recent	8B	responsible	3B
▲reclaim	5B	retire	7A
recognize	4B	▲revival	6A
recovery	6A	▲revive	6A
▲recreation	7A	revolution	8A
▲recreational	7A	▲revolutionize	8A
▲referee	3A	rewarding	2B
regarding	1A	right	7B
relate	5A	role	4B
related	4A	roughly	8A
▲relationship	5A	ruin	6A
relative	7B	rule	3B
relax	1B		

S

save	6B	secret	1A
▲savvy	8B	section	3B
scale	6A	seek	6A
scholarship	2B	sense	1B
schooler	2A	series	1B
scientist	8A	serve	8A
★screw	3B	several	3A
search	6A	shape	2A
★secondary	2A	share	5B

T

theater	7B	towards	3B
★therefore	4B	★track	6B
think	2B	★traffic	8B
thousand	3A	treatment	3B
tired	7B	trial	4A
together	7A	trip	7B
★topic	1A	truck	2B
total	6A	trust	5A

U

unacceptable	1A	★university	2B
uncomfortable	1A	until	2A
uncover	6A	up	3B
★underestimate	8A	use	7A
★unexpected	4B	usually	3A
unhealthy	3A		

V

★value	1A	★via	8B
★vary	3A	★video	7B

W

watch	2B	willing	4B
★wealth	8B	win	6B
weather	1A	winner	4B
week	7A	wisely	7A
weekday	7B	wise	7A
weekend	2B	wish	2B
★weigh	3A	without	5A
★weight	3A	wonderful	2A
wheel	6B	★workshop	6B
whether	7A	world	6A
▲whine	3B	worry	3A

教师信息反馈表

为了更好地为教师服务,提高教学质量,我社将为您的教学提供电子和网络支持。请您填好以下表格并经系主任签字盖章后寄回,我社将免费向您提供相关的电子教案、网络交流平台或网络化课程资源。

书名:			版次	
书号:				
所需要的教学资料:				
您的姓名:				
您所在的校(院)、系:		校(院)		系
您所讲授的课程名称:				
学生人数:	_____人 _____年级	学时:		
您的联系地址:				
邮政编码:		联系电话		(家)
				(手机)
E-mail:(必填)				
您对本书的建议:		系主任签字 盖章		

请寄:重庆市沙坪坝正街 174 号重庆大学(A 区)

重庆大学出版社市场部

邮编:400030

电话:023-65111124

传真:023-65103686

网址:http://www.cqup.com.cn

E-mail:fxk@cqup.com.cn